S0-BEC-725

"I'm forbidden fruit," Tessa warned him, laughing

Alaric was laughing, too, a low, deep laugh that caught at her memory. "Thanks for the information. You're a girl who says no, are you?"

"Correct," said Tessa crisply, and saw that in spite of the traffic he slid a quick glance toward her. She kept her eyes resolutely ahead. "What's our route?" she inquired, changing the subject pointedly. "I don't suppose you need me to navigate?"

"Oh, no, thanks. I could find my way blindfolded," he said. "And I could think of much better uses to put you to, Tessa."

"Like taking a job as a chemist in your new lab?"

"We-ell," he mused, "let's say chemistry comes into it."

Marjorie Lewty is a born romantic. "It's all in the way you look at the world," she suggests. "Maybe if I hadn't been lucky enough to find love myself—in my parents, my husband, my children—I might have viewed the world with cynicism." As it is, she writes about "what is surely the most important and exciting part of growing up, and that is falling in love." She and her family live in Leamington, a pleasant town full of beautiful parks and old Georgian homes.

Books by Marjorie Lewty

HARLEQUIN ROMANCE

HARLEQUIN PRESENTS

Don't miss any of our special offers. Write to us at the following address for information on our newest releases.

Harlequin Reader Service
901 Fuhrmann Blvd., P.O. Box 1397, Buffalo, NY 14240
Canadian address: P.O. Box 603,
Fort Erie, Ont. L2A 5X3

Falling in Love Again

Marjorie Lewty

Harlequin Books

TORONTO • NEW YORK • LONDON
AMSTERDAM • PARIS • SYDNEY • HAMBURG
STOCKHOLM • ATHENS • TOKYO • MILAN

Original hardcover edition published in 1988
by Mills & Boon Limited

ISBN 0-373-17032-7

Harlequin Romance first edition February 1989

Copyright © 1988 by Marjorie Lewty.
All rights reserved. Except for use in any review, the reproduction or utilization
of this work in whole or in part in any form by any electronic, mechanical or
other means, now known or hereafter invented, including xerography,
photocopying and recording, or in any information storage or retrieval system,
is forbidden without the permission of the publisher, Harlequin Enterprises
Limited, 225 Duncan Mill Road, Don Mills, Ontario, Canada M3B 3K9.

All the characters in this book have no existence outside the imagination of
the author and have no relation whatsoever to anyone bearing the same name
or names. They are not even distantly inspired by any individual known or
unknown to the author, and all incidents are pure invention.

® are Trademarks registered in the United States Patent and Trademark Office
and in other countries.

Printed in U.S.A.

CHAPTER ONE

ON AN afternoon in early June Miss Carter, martinet of the typing-pool, stomped into the general office of Brent Pharmaceuticals plc, and passed a flinty eye over the rows of electronic typewriters and their flagging operators.

'Miss Fowkes and Miss Durant. You're both to go up to Mr Alaric Brent's office—immediately, please.'

Freda Fowkes's round blue eyes opened wide as she pushed back her typing chair eagerly. 'Wow!' she mouthed under her breath, as she reached Tessa Durant's desk. 'Come on, Tessa.'

Tessa followed Freda out to the lift. The two girls could hardly have been less alike. Freda Fowkes was small and cheerfully plump with pink cheeks and curly brown hair. She hurried along the corridor, two paces ahead of the taller, more slender Tessa. Tessa wore her dark, satin-smooth hair taken back from her face and knotted behind her small, well shaped head. Her big green eyes surveyed the world around her with cool appraisal from under long, curving lashes. Her rather exquisite mouth always looked as if it were on the verge of smiling. Which was misleading, because Tessa Durant hadn't done much smiling for quite a time.

In the lift Tessa frowned puzzledly. 'I didn't know we'd committed any awful crimes, did you, Freda? Why are we being carpeted, do you think?'

Freda was running a pocket comb frantically through her curls. 'You've got the wrong idea, Tess. I've heard that our Alaric's needing a temp. secretary while Brenda Johnson goes on three months' leave to have her baby. Golly, what an opportunity!'

'Is it?' Tessa's pale face registered nothing more than mild interest. 'Well, I hope he chooses you, Freda. I'm quite happy where I am.'

'What?' Freda's blue eyes popped. 'You can't be serious. Have you seen the man? No, I don't suppose you have, he's been away in Dorset for months, setting up the new lab there, he probably went before you joined the firm. He's a real stunner.' She raised her eyes to the ceiling of the lift that was bearing them up to the fifth floor.

Tessa smiled and shrugged. 'I'm not sure I take to stunners.'

The other girl stuffed her comb away as the lift came smoothly to a halt at the fifth floor. 'Wait till you see him,' she chuckled, and then composed her features into a decorous expression as the two girls stepped out into the hushed atmosphere of the carpeted corridor. 'It's like being in church up here,' Freda whispered.

Discreet plates on the doors announced the names of the occupants. Tessa, who had joined the firm two months ago, working in the typing-pool, was familiar with only one or two of them. James A. Marlor, General Manager, through whom she had got her job—on the recommendation of Tom Jarvis, who was a friend of Mr Marlor's. Frederick Dunn, Personnel Manager, who had also interviewed her and was pleasant and helpful. Miss Cara Everett, Company Secretary. No, Tessa hadn't met her.

'Here we go,' murmured Freda reverently, as they stopped outside a door marked 'A.J.Brent, Director'. She tapped and waited.

A feminine voice from inside called, 'Come in,' and they entered an outer office where a red-haired girl in large glasses, whom Tessa knew slightly as Brenda Johnson, one of the top secretaries, sat behind a desk in the corner. She smiled at them amiably. 'Hullo, Freda—Tessa—ready for the fray?' She gestured towards the communicating door. 'You'd better go in first, Freda. You sit down over there and wait, Tessa.'

Tessa took the chair indicated and awaited events. The secretary pressed a switch on the intercom. 'Miss Fowkes is here to see you, sir.' A deep voice growled something unintelligible. 'In you go,' Brenda said to Freda.

Tessa was amused to see how Freda's pink cheeks had gone suddenly pale, how her hand was shaking as she tapped at the door before she disappeared into the inner office. She supposed that if the job had meant a lot to her, she herself would have been all of a flutter. It was a sort of negative bonus that she didn't care. One day, perhaps, she would begin to get enthusiastic about a career as a secretary, but not yet. It was too soon, and when you're frozen inside you don't feel much emotion about anything.

Brenda was looking at her rather curiously. 'You

must have been pleased to be picked for an interview, weren't you?' I mean, you haven't been working for the company long. Mr Marlor was singing your praises to me the other day. He seems to think you rate something different from the typing-pool.'

Tessa smiled composedly. 'Nice of him,' she murmured.

When she didn't volunteer anything further Brenda shrugged and turned back to her desk. A funny girl, Tessa Durant. Not stuck-up or unfriendly, just not outgoing. And she often looked sort of faraway. Probably man-trouble, Brenda decided knowingly. Tessa was a pretty girl, the kind who drew men like a magnet. Although 'pretty' wasn't quite the right word. Lovely, really, with her fine, dark hair and enormous green eyes and the high cheekbones that threw shadows on to cheeks that were pale and thin. Too pale and thin. Yes, undoubtedly man-trouble, Brenda decided, putting a fresh sheet of paper in her typewriter.

When Freda emerged, ten minutes later, her face was several shades pinker than usual and she was breathing rather fast as she slipped into a chair next to Tessa. 'Your turn now, chum,' she murmured. 'Go on, he's waiting for you.'

The director's office was half the size of a tennis court, with plate-glass windows looking across the city of London. The late afternoon sunlight was dazzling as Tessa made her way across acres of dove-grey carpet to where a man sat behind an enormous desk with his back to the window.

'Sit down,' Miss Durant,' said a deep, courteous voice and Tessa sat in the chair opposite, waiting for him to look up from the papers on his desk. When he did she drew in her breath in a little gasp. At first, with the light in her eyes, she hadn't seen him clearly, but now she did she felt a shock-wave passing through her because it might almost have been Marc sitting facing her across the desk. The same thick brown hair, the same lazy droop of eyelids over storm-grey eyes. Marc had had only to smile at her under those lowered eyelids to turn her knees to jelly.

But the man on the other side of the desk wasn't smiling and she tried to concentrate on what he was saying.

'—know you've only been with the firm a short time, but Mr Marlor put in a word for you in connection with a vacancy that's coming up in Dorset. As you may know, we're setting up a new laboratory there. The conversion and fitting is almost complete and we hope to be operational in a week or two. Before I go into any detail, how does the idea of moving out into the country—seaside, really—appeal to you?'

Tessa fixed her eyes on the window behind his shoulder. Her heart was still thudding unpleasantly, but she mustn't make a fool of herself. 'I—er—hadn't thought about it.'

'Have you any ties that would make it difficult for you to be away from London for a time?'

'Er—no, that is, I mean, I——'

Alaric Brent frowned. An efficient young lady, Jimmy Marlor had said. Keen, intelligent, not a clock-watcher. Well qualified, too. She had sounded just what he needed. Then why was she stammering like a nervous schoolgirl? Any why wouldn't she meet his eyes?'

Tessa made herself glance at the man sitting across the desk and then immediately her eyes slid away again. 'I'm sorry, Mr Brent,' she said and was relieved to hear that her voice had almost regained the cool steadiness she had been practising for months. 'It just took me by surprise. I hadn't realised that the job would mean leaving London.'

'Ah, I see. The boyfriend wouldn't stand for it, I suppose?'

She shook her head. 'Nothing like that.'

She met his eyes for a moment and then looked away again. She was being very stupid, and over-reacting. This could be a good job and lead to a higher position in the company. She needed experience if she were ever to make a career as a secretary. She needed enthusiasm, too, and so far secretarial work had seemed dull and undemanding after her chosen work—the work she had been trained for. Alaric Brent was a top man in the company, he would be forceful and demanding and stretch her to the limit. Which would certainly be good for her. But could she work with a man who was so disturbingly like Marc, who would remind her constantly? And to work in a research laboratory! To be so close to the work she loved and yet not be part of it!

'Well, Miss Durant?' He sounded a trifle impatient now.

'You mean—are you offering me the job, Mr Brent?'

He nodded. 'On Mr Marlor's recommendation—yes. I value his opinion highly. On a month's trial, to see how you get along. What about it?' He smiled at her, his teeth white against sun-bronzed skin.

Marc used to smile at her like that—when he wanted her to do something for him. She could never refuse him anything—fool that she had been.

There was a silence and Alaric Brent studied her face, dark brows raised. Then he said, 'Perhaps you have taken a dislike to me on sight?'

She looked up quickly. Sarcasm? But no, he was still smiling, and she smiled back nervously. 'Of course not, why should I dislike you?'

'Why indeed?' he said drily.

She wondered what he would say if she told him the truth. If she said, 'I can't look at you without seeing Marc looking back at me. I know I'm being very silly and you're probably not in the least like Marc, except for your looks, but you remind me—and I want so desperately to forget. Working as your secretary—seeing you every day—I don't think I could do it.'

She said, 'I do appreciate your offering me the job, Mr Brent. It's just that I—I was engaged as a typist and I haven't had any experience yet of real secretarial work. I'd be afraid of falling short of what you need.'

'Secretarial work? Who said anything about secretarial work? Didn't Miss Carter brief you before she sent you up here?'

Tessa's green eyes widened. 'She just told Freda and me to come up to see you. Freda said she'd heard you were looking for a temporary secretary.'

The long straight mouth pulled down in annoyance. 'Then Miss Carter has evidently slipped up yet again. Well, to put the record straight, Miss Durant, the secretarial job is already filled—by Miss Fowkes. The appointment on offer to you is one that should appeal to you—as a trained research chemist.'

Tessa gasped. 'Chemist?'

He raised his eyebrows. 'Don't look so horrified—it isn't a dark secret, surely? It's all here in the records.' He tapped the papers on his desk.

Tessa stared with fascinated horror at the typed form. Upside down and across the wide desk the words were quite undecipherable. All here, he had said. But it couldn't be all there—not the damning details of the reason she had left—been ignominiously sacked from—Ferris Knight in Birmingham. Alaric Brent wouldn't be offering her a job as a chemist if he knew about that.

He looked down again at the top sheet of paper. 'You were introduced to us by Mr Thomas Jarvis, head chemist at Ferris Knight in Birmingham, who is a friend of our general manager, Mr Marlor. You'd given up your job with Ferris Knight due to illness after a car accident. When you finally recovered, some months later, you decided to change to secretarial work—for which you had had previous training—and we took you on in that capacity. We don't usually appoint staff without a written reference, but as you hadn't worked at Ferris Knight for some months, and then not on the secretarial side, and as Mr Jarvis vouched for your integrity, we didn't contact them.'

'I see.' A small flicker of hope began to stir inside

Tessa. Perhaps she was going to be allowed to return to working at her beloved chemistry after all!

The man opposite was looking keenly at her. 'Why did you give up laboratory work, Miss Durant? Surely it was more interesting than typing?'

She didn't have to answer him, but the subtle magnetism was working. As she met those storm-grey eyes she felt the pull of a dynamic personality. Marc had been dynamic too; ambitious, thrusting, a man on his way to the top in the shortest possible time.

'I wanted a change,' she said quietly. 'I'd had a long, trying illness and I thought that secretarial work would be less—demanding.'

'I see,' he said slowly, and she hoped he didn't. The trauma of the Ferris Knight affair was in the past—just as Marc was in the past. And that was where it must stay.

'Well now,' he said, suddenly brisk. 'Let me tell you something about our new venture. This is my "baby" and I'm keeping it quite separate from all our other activities. As I expect you know, up to now our line has been purely the manufacture of synthetically produced drugs. My own interest is research into natural remedies derived from plants.'

He got up and walked to the window and stood looking out. He was very tall, over six feet, Tessa guessed. Taller than Marc, and broader. In his well tailored dark suit he exuded an air of confidence, almost of arrogance. A very masculine man, his very existence issuing an immediate sexual challenge to a woman without his even trying. Life would have its complications for him, Tessa thought, wondering if he was married. Women would flock around him like bees round a honey-pot. Not her though, Tessa thought, a little smile curling her lip. Alaric Brent was the very picture of the type of man she intended to avoid in future. But what on earth was she thinking of? This was a business interview, for heaven's sake; there was nothing personal about it.

He had turned from the window and was pacing up and down in front of his desk, stopping now and again to meet her eyes as he emphasised a point. 'You know, it's a fascinating idea that there isn't a single disease in man that may not be remedied or cured by some plant or herb. You only have to watch the way animals seek out a particular plant when they're ill. They keep the ancient intuitive knowledge to guide them—knowledge that we've lost. Traditional Chinese medicine uses hundreds of plant remedies but in the crude form. Of course, many modern drugs already use plants as their raw material, but I believe there is enormous progress to be made in the analysis of all sorts of previously untested plants for their medicinal value. It's a thrilling prospect, a lifetime's work. I can't wait to get started.'

Tessa found herself watching Alaric Brent's face, seeing there a zest and enthusiasm that struck a chord in her.

'There's been a good deal of research done in the last twenty or twenty-five years,' he went on. 'In the US and in Switzerland. And of course there are many herbalists practising. But this is something a little different. If we come up with something good Brent Pharmaceuticals will market it on an international scale. This is the sort of work we're going to do at the new lab in Dorset. It's right off the beaten track there—we don't want to advertise what we're doing. Also, it happens to be my favourite part of the country. I've got a hand-picked team together, but one of the assistant chemists has dropped out—her family is emigrating and she's going with them.'

He sat down again in his leather director's chair. 'That's where you might come in, Miss Durant. Are you interested?' The smoke-grey eyes were fixed keenly on her face.

'Oh, yes, I am.' She was more than interested, she was suddenly excited. It would be wonderful to get back to her own chosen work. But what if all the old scandal in Birmingham came out? Could she risk losing everything again?

She said guardedly, 'It sounds fascinating. But—wouldn't you want someone with more experience? I was only doing a very minor sort of job with Ferris Knight.' Marc had been the leader of their two-person team; she had merely been his assistant, learning from him, worshipping him as a scientist, as a man, as a lover——

'Oh, we can forget about your job with Ferris Knight.' Alaric Brent brushed that aside. 'You're a graduate, I know that from your records, and that's good enough for me. Also, you've been working for us for some months, and I hope—I'm sure—that you can give your loyalty to the company. This is confidential work and I would prefer to give the job to someone inside the company, rather than bring in an outsider.'

He sat back in his chair. 'I've given you just an

outline of the project. I'd like you to have a look round the new lab and the district before you make up your mind. Would tomorrow be convenient for you? I'm driving down myself, making an early start because I have to be back here for a directors' meeting in the afternoon.' He frowned slightly. 'That's another hurdle I have to cross. I've been delegating too much of my work in London lately.'

Tessa stood up. Trying to sound casual, she said, 'You don't intend to make your headquarters in Dorset, then?'

'Oh lord, no, much as I'd like to. Now, about tomorrow. You'd better give me your address and phone number. I'll pick you up early, about half seven—that OK with you?' He took out a notebook and looked at her questioningly.

Tessa's head was spinning. 'You've rather taken my breath away.' It was so tempting—so very, very tempting. To get away from London to the country, where the air was pure and the wind whipped at your cheeks, blowing away old miseries. To exchange a dusty office for the immaculate cleanliness of a laboratory. To work again in a discipline she loved. To make a completely new start. And she wouldn't even have this man there to remind her of Marc. It could be the very last chance she would have to get back into her chosen profession. She just *had* to take the risk that the reason for her leaving Ferris Knight would be discovered. But still she hesitated.

'Well?' Alaric Brent was watching her closely. He sounded really impatient now.

'Yes, thank you,' Tessa said. 'I'd like to come.'

'Good,' he said briskly, pencil poised over his notebook. 'The address, then.'

He wrote it down as she dictated and then walked with her to the door. Tessa wasn't a small girl, but he towered over her. His size and closeness made her feel slightly dizzy.

'I'll see you in the morning then, Miss Durant. Tessa, isn't it?'

He smiled down at her. He had a heart-stopping smile—*and* he was no doubt aware of it. She reached for the door-handle but his hand was there first and his fingers brushed hers. A shiver passed through her, up her arm and down her body. It was as if Marc had reached out and touched her: the same immediate unbidden thrill of recognition, the same body chemistry that she had never expected to experience again.

'OK?' he said, opening the door.

She nodded. 'OK,' she muttered, and hurried through the outer office to the corridor, not noticing Brenda Johnson's surprised glance that followed her escape.

Tessa didn't wait for the lift, she ran down the stairs to the girls' room on the third floor. She needed to be alone for a few minutes to get over the interview with Alaric Brent. What had happened had been so absolutely unexpected. Now that she was away from the magnetic field that that man seemed to set up round himself, she wondered if she had been crazy to agree to travel down to Dorset tomorrow with him. It was all in the way of business, of course, it was laughable to imagine that he would have any sinister intentions, but all the same—his likeness to Marc had had an unnerving effect on her and she felt disturbed and apprehensive. If she could be thrown off balance by just seeing and talking to a man who reminded her so poignantly of Marc, how in the world was she going to put that old trauma behind her for good? As she pushed open the door of the girls' room she had an urge to go back upstairs, to tell Alaric Brent that she had changed her mind——

'Hello, Tessa, we meet again.' Freda Fowkes raised a dripping face from one of the row of wash-basins. 'Needed to cool off after all the excitement,' she explained, dabbing her flushed cheeks with a paper towel.

'You got the job?' That was fairly obvious—Freda was fairly glowing with satisfaction.

'And how!' Freda met Tessa's eyes in the mirror and her mouth pulled down apologetically. 'Sorry, chum, but one of us had to win. And you weren't all that keen, were you?' she added rather anxiously.

Tessa smiled reassuringly. 'Don't worry. It seems Miss Carter slipped up. She didn't tell us that there were two jobs on offer. I got the other one. Snap!'

'Oh goody, I'm so glad.' Freda rummaged in the tote bag in her locker and produced a weekly magazine. 'I just knew something good was going to happen today. Just listen to this: "Gemini—The golden sun rides high in your house of career this week. You are active and industrious and like interesting and varied work, so direct your ambitions positively."' She waved the magazine in the air triumphantly. 'How about that then? You're not a

Gemini, are you Tessa?'

'No—Libra,' Tessa said.

Freda ran a finger down the column and read, 'Libra—you have a great feeling for balance which sometimes makes it hard for you to come to a decision. But this is one time when you must be positive, so go to it and you won't have any regrets.'

Suddenly Tessa felt a rush of excitement to match Freda's. She had never placed the faith in magazine horoscopes that Freda did, but this one had certainly hit the nail on the head. Of course she wouldn't turn down the opportunity of such a marvellous job—whatever had she been thinking of even to contemplate doing so?

Freda was looking a little puzzled. 'I still can't see how there are *two* jobs. Surely the man doesn't need two secretaries? Although I wouldn't be surprised if his work-load would run to that. Brenda Johnson says he's a glutton for work.'

Tessa shook her head, smiling. 'This is where I put on my other hat. I used to work in a laboratory—assistant chemist—and that's the job he wants me for. In the new lab in Dorset.'

'Well!' Freda took a bottle of skin-lotion from her handbag. 'Aren't you the dark horse, then? Will you enjoy it?'

'Oh, *yes.*' Tessa washed her hands, noticing from her reflection in the mirror that her green eyes were shining. It was a long time since they had shone like that. 'It's what I want more than anything.'

'More than working with Sexy Alaric?' Freda giggled. 'You won't see much of him—seems he's coming back to London now the lab in Dorset's nearly finished. He's a real dish, isn't he? Not that a mere secretary would have much hope. Brenda was telling me that he isn't married but that Cara Everett has got her claws well and truly stuck in. You know her—the company secretary. Wears trendy gear, not at all suitable for a top executive, Brenda says. Have a dab.' Freda held out the bottle of skin-tonic. 'Apparently she was always turning up when Alaric was down in Dorset. It'll be fun to see how the big romance proceeds. I'll ring you up and keep you posted.'

Tessa applied the cool, fragrant liquid gratefully to her cheeks and forehead. 'Thanks, Freda, that was lovely. Come on, we'd better get back or the Carter will be creating.'

And the two girls hurried down the stairs to the general office, each of them, in her own way, feeling very pleased with life.

Tessa was still feeling euphoric when she let herself into her flat that evening. 'Flat' was paying a compliment to the small bed-sitter with kitchenette and shared bathroom in Muswell Hill, but it was all she could afford on her salary. When she came to London her parents had offered to help out. 'It's so poky,' her mother had said in dismay, on her first visit from Devon. 'After that nice flat you had in Birmingham when you first went to work there—oh dear, I shouldn't have reminded you of that, I'm sorry, love.'

'Flats are cheaper in Birmingham,' Tessa said sharply. Then, seeing her mother's hurt face, she added, 'Don't worry, Mum, all that's in the past now, this is a new start, and I've got to begin at the bottom again.'

Mary Durant sighed. 'I suppose so. How are you getting on with your new colleagues? Is there anyone specially nice there?'

For 'specially nice' read 'eligible young men', Tessa thought wryly. Mary Durant was the best of mothers, but, like all mothers, wanted to see her daughter nicely settled down with the right man. Especially after Marc, of course. Her mother had never liked Marc. When the engagement was announced and Tessa took him to visit her parents at their retirement bungalow in Devon he hadn't really wanted to go, and certainly hadn't put himself out to charm her parents. He was in one of his sulky moods all weekend and the visit had been a disaster.

Tessa and her mother had got as near to quarrelling about him as they had ever got about anything. But when, two months later, it ended so tragically there had been no 'I-told-you-so's'. Only love and compassion and unfailing support, and for that Tessa would always be grateful.

This evening the flat was even less like a desirable residence than usual. The June day had been hot and the house felt stuffy. Someone downstairs had been cooking smoked fish; the bath was festooned with a row of tights and stockings; and as Tessa opened the window of her room the hot, dusty air from the street wafted in despondently. Oh, to get away from all this to the green of the countryside, to work in a laboratory again! It seemed like a glimpse of heaven and she couldn't imagine why she had hesitated for a second.

But after every 'high' there must inevitably come a 'low', and Tessa's 'low' came as she was lying in bed that night, too excited to go to sleep.

Alaric Brent had said they wouldn't approach Ferris Knight for a reference but how could she be sure?

She went cold as she imagined the anger and contempt in his eyes if he should ever find out that she had kept from him the fact that she had been dismissed from the Ferris Knight company for 'gross negligence and incompetence'. But surely she was justified in keeping the whole wretched business to herself, she argued. After all, she was innocent—the fault hadn't been hers, it had been Marc's.

She wished now that she had taken Tom Jarvis's advice, when he came to see her after Marc's death, and had gone to the Ferris Knight directors with the true story, as Tom urged her to do. But she hadn't, she had been too sick at heart to pursue the matter, and now it was too late to do anything about it, and anyway Tom would have been retired by now. He was just about to retire when it all happened. The past had caught up with her and got tangled with the present.

She tossed and turned, trying to relax, but her head was full of memories, right back to where it all started. Leaving the university with a good degree and delighted with the offer of a job with Ferris Knight, a smallish chemical company in the Midlands. Meeting Marc Nichols and feeling thrilled at the prospect of working with him. Marc—tall and dark and devastatingly attractive. Brilliant at his job, drivingly ambitious, and with so much charm that inside a week Tessa was hopelessly in love with him.

From this distance of time she saw how young and inexperienced she had been at twenty-two. She had been a dedicated student—utterly engrossed with her work, never tempted to experiment seriously with boys, laughing off her friends' jibes about being a hopeless romantic.

But now she met Marc Nichols and all her newly-discovered passionate nature took over. When, a few weeks later, Marc asked her to give up her flat and move in with him she agreed with hardly a backward glance. 'We'll see how it works, darling,' he'd promised. 'If we get along, maybe we'll get married.'

Tessa never had a doubt that they would get along. Utterly obsessed with Marc, she lived to please him. Nobody had told her that, by and large, men get tired of willing slaves. In the daytime they worked together at the laboratory. In the evenings Tessa cooked, and cleaned the flat. She washed and ironed his shirts and still managed to look good when Marc and she went to parties together. And she never tired of his lovemaking. She discovered in herself a passion that she had never suspected, and their nights were full of delirious magic for Tessa. And Marc was satisfied, she was sure he was. 'You're the most wonderful thing that ever happened to me,' he groaned as they clung together, their bodies silky damp, their limbs entwined.

Oh yes, she would be the perfect wife, she would make life so good for him that he would never need anyone else.

Looking back now, she wondered what would have happened if things had gone right with his work at the lab, instead of so terribly, terribly wrong. .

The day it happened was engraved on her memory. Marc had been working for months on a research project that was going to shoot up his reputation in the firm when it turned out successfully. All had been going well, the end was in sight and he was euphoric about it. Then—horrors—one small experiment came up with the wrong answer.

'It can't be, it can't possibly be wrong.' She saw his face again, pale and set in the bright laboratory lights, as he stared disbelievingly at the computer screen. 'Work through it again, Tessa. Even if we stay here all night we've got to get it right.'

Three times they repeated the stage of the experiment and three times it came out the same.

Marc ran despairing fingers through his hair. 'God, Tessa,' he groaned. 'You know what this means—all my work for the last eight months down the drain!'

Then his face changed, his mouth was a thin, straight line, his eyes narrowed into an expression that Tessa had never seen before. 'You get along home, Tessa,' he said. 'Leave it to me. I'll bust this block if it kills me. Don't wait up for me.'

She had argued a little with him, not wanting to leave him in this mood, trying to persuade him to try again tomorrow, but he had suddenly shouted at her violently, 'Get out—go on, get out when I tell you. Leave me alone.'

So, trembling with tiredness and fear of a side of Marc she had never seen before, Tessa did as he told her. She was still awake at two o'clock in the morning when he came in, white and utterly exhausted. She mixed him a whisky and he tossed it down, peeling off his clothes. 'How did it——' she ventured. 'Did it go right in the end?'

He smiled at her, a smile that wasn't a smile at all, but a grimace of a man at the end of his tether. 'Oh yes, it went right in the end,' he said and fell into bed and into a deep sleep that lasted until noon the next day.

The research project was hailed by the firm as a spectacular breakthrough. Marc's reputation soared, there was talk of his being given his own department. Tests of the new drug were put under way.

It was some weeks later when the blow fell. Tom Jarvis, head of research, called Marc into his office and they were closeted there for hours. Marc's face was grim when he emerged. 'Let's go out for lunch,' he said to Tessa. 'We have to talk.'

At a corner table in their usual café he told her what had happened. At first she could hardly believe it, but in the end she had to. Marc had done what no scientist should do: he had deliberately skipped a vital stage when the result came out inexplicably wrong. He thought he knew what the answer should be and, impatient for results, he had entered that in the computer instead of going back and repeating months of work from the very beginning.

'I was so *sure*,' he groaned. 'I thought it must be some little mistake—a mistake that probably you had made.'

'Me?' Tessa gasped. 'How could it have been me?

You checked everything I did.'

He looked strangely at her across the table, with its
yellow formica top and its half-empty coffee mugs.
'But what if I hadn't?' he said softly. 'What if you'd
gone on alone and forgotten to consult me? What if
you'd just entered a result off your own bat? Perhaps
when I wasn't there. Then I couldn't be blamed,
could I?'

Tessa met his eyes, saw the desperation in them.
She was suddenly cold all over as she realised what
he was asking of her. To take the blame on
herself—almost certainly to be sacked in disgrace.

'Oh, I couldn't——' she began.

'It would never happen again, Tess,' he promised,
very low. 'I've learned my lesson for all time. And
would it matter so very much to you? We'd be
married—have kids—that's what you've always
wanted, isn't it?' His voice grew urgent as he sensed
the weakening in her. He leaned across the café table,
pleading with her. 'Oh, Tessa, my darling, I'm
imploring your help. I need you so terribly. My whole
career—my whole life—is in your hands.'

She loved him deeply and there was only one
answer. All through the nightmare days that followed
she hung on to the one thought—that she had saved
Marc.

When it was over and Tessa had been dismissed,
while Marc had been cleared of all suspicion, his
gratitude knew no bounds. They became engaged, she
took Marc to meet her parents. She enrolled for a
secretarial course because her work in the small flat
couldn't possibly fill all her time, and there was no

hope of her finding another job in research chemistry. Who would give her a job without a reference?

The date for the wedding wasn't yet fixed and Tessa told herself to ignore the tiny doubts that were creeping in. She didn't know that guilt can poison any relationship, she only knew that things between herself and Marc weren't the same. He began to have silent moods when she couldn't reach him, and snapped irritably at her when she tried.

It was a shock, and yet almost a relief, when she found she was pregnant. She left the doctor's surgery that afternoon and wandered round the streets, longing to see Marc, to tell him, to hear him say, 'Sweetheart, that's great. We'll get married straight away.' She couldn't bear to go back to the flat and wait there alone for him to come in. He had been very late coming home some nights recently. He told her he had started on a new and important piece of research.

At last, when she could keep the news to herself no longer, she ventured back to the laboratory for the first time since she left there in disgrace. That was when she saw Marc come out with his new girl assistant, saw them go into 'their' little café—Tessa's and Marc's. Saw the way Marc looked across the table at the girl with the brown bobbed hair and cheeky little nose. Saw him press her hand across the table. And the blood in her body turned to ice.

Even now, all those months later, Tessa felt deathly cold as she huddled under the bedclothes, forcing herself for the first time to face everything that had happened after that. How Marc had been furious about the baby, had blamed her and accused her of trying to trap him into marriage. How he had raged at her when she wouldn't agree to what he called a 'termination'.

Tessa's world had collapsed around her. Dumbly she agreed when he told her that she had better go home to her parents in Devon. She watched while he flung her bags into the car, his face set into a sullen scowl. She didn't know this Marc—had never known him. She sat in frozen silence beside him in the car while the rain streamed down the windscreen and Marc drove furiously along the motorway, his mouth set into a hard line, silent, hostile, ignoring speed limits and the caution needed to cope with the weather conditions.

Now, lying huddled in bed, she was living it again, that terrible drive, hearing the scream of brakes, seeing the great black shape of a lorry close in front of the car. Too close. Hearing again her own muffled shriek. And then—nothing.

It was like a nightmare, only it wasn't a nightmare, it was remembered reality. She drew the bedclothes round her frantically, her body damp with sweat, her heart thudding against her ribs, the taste of salt tears on her lips.

But presently the shivering stopped, her heartbeat slowed. She stumbled across the room to the washbasin and swilled her face in cool water and pushed back her tangled hair. She got back into bed and stretched out flat and presently she began to feel curiously calm. Making herself remember instead of suppressing the painful events of nearly a year ago seemed to have released a locked-up load of misery inside her and left her feeling freer and lighter than she had done for ages.

She *could* make a new start. The job that Alaric Brent had offered her sounded exactly what she wanted, and she would be incredibly lucky to get it. She had to make herself believe that he had meant what he said when he told her he didn't intend to approach Ferris Knight for a reference.

As for Alaric Brent himself—yes, he was a dangerously attractive man—yes, he was extraordinarily like Marc. But if she was going to allow herself to be disturbed by every man she met who had thick brown hair and smoke-grey eyes and a habit of twisting his mouth and smiling a lazy smile under long lashes, then she was going to let herself in for a great deal of disappointment, she decided with a flash of humour. Anyway, Alaric Brent wouldn't be around very much at the new lab, he had told her that.

And, as Freda had discovered, he had an elegant and snooty girlfriend who was the company secretary, so he wouldn't be likely to be looking *her* way. He had offered her the job because he needed another chemist for his new lab. That was all.

No more dithering, she was going to take the job and work hard and establish herself on the research side of Brent's. Desperately tired, but with the optimism that follows on making a firm decision, Tessa settled down to sleep.

She couldn't wait for tomorrow to come.

CHAPTER TWO

TESSA was up at six o'clock next morning, after a ragged night. She made coffee and forced herself to eat a piece of toast. One bonus that came with early rising was getting the bathroom to herself. She had a leisurely bath in tepid water. Then, taking her time, she dressed in a neat suit of navy and white check with a white blouse, which seemed to fit the occasion and look businesslike. She brushed her dark, shoulder-length hair until it shone like satin and arranged it in a pleat at the back of her head, applied light shadow to her eyes, trying to cover the tell-tale signs of the previous night, brushed on lipgloss sparingly and examined her pale cheeks. A blusher? No, she didn't think so. The object of the exercise was merely to look neat and well groomed, not to impress Alaric Brent. It wouldn't matter to him whether she looked eye-catching—far more important that she should present the picture of a confident young professional woman.

She was ready soon after seven and stationed herself beside the window, looking down over the suburban road with its rows of cars parked nose to tail along both sides. She would see Alaric Brent's car as soon as it appeared and run down the stairs to join him. Her heart was beginning to beat rather uncomfortably fast at the prospect of seeing him again and she concentrated on breathing slowly and evenly, as she had been taught in hospital after the accident, to get herself reasonably relaxed before she had to see Alaric Brent again. This time she would be prepared and wouldn't be thrown off balance by his likeness to Marc.

When he hadn't appeared by a quarter to eight she began to get jittery. Had he changed his mind about offering her the job? Had someone with better experience turned up? Worst of all, had he found out about her reason for leaving Ferris Knight?

She went down to the front door and stood looking up and down the road. Another quarter of an hour dragged past, minute by minute. The church clock struck eight slowly and ominously. No, he wasn't coming now. He must have changed his mind. Tessa felt quite sick with disappointment.

Then suddenly the phone burred in the hall behind her, and old Mrs Rawlings, from the bottom flat, opened her door.

'OK, I'll get it.' Tessa rushed to the wall-hung phone and grabbed the receiver, her hand shaking. 'Hello?'

'Tessa? This is Alaric Brent.' The deep voice sounded exactly the same on the phone as if he were here before her, and her mouth went dry.

'Oh yes, hello,' she croaked.

'Look, Tessa, it's a damned nuisance but I can't get away yet. Something's come up and the meeting has had to be put forward. It'll probably be after midday before I can get away. Which means that by the time our business in Dorset is over it'll be too late to get back to London tonight. I've rung Barney Grant—he's my head man at the new lab. He and his wife have moved into a

cottage quite near—and they would be delighted to put
you up. So I suggest that you pack an overnight bag and
I'll call for you as soon as I can get away. That suit you?'

Tessa felt quite weak with relief. So the job wasn't off
after all. Marvellous—wonderful! 'Yes, thank you, that
suits me fine.' she said calmly. 'I'll be ready for you.'

'Good girl,' he said and the phone went dead.

As she replaced the receiver she saw Mrs Rawlings
hovering in her doorway, a knitted cardigan draped over
her flannelette nightdress. Mrs Rawlings was a good
soul, but, with nothing to do but interest herself in the
affairs of the other tenants, she could get extremely
irritating at times. 'OK, dear?' she enquired curiously.

At this moment even Mrs Rawlings couldn't shake
Tessa's elation.

She nodded, beaming at the old lady. 'OK, thanks.'

OK. Very much OK. She hummed a song as she
raced back up the stairs two at a time to her room and
lugged down a small case from the top of the wardrobe.
She would need a light dress to wear this evening if she
was staying with these people called Grant. The yellow
seersucker one with the white polka dots and plain
yellow bolero was the nicest she had. She had bought it
for that holiday in Rhodes that she and Marc had
planned, but the holiday hadn't come off. Marc had
decided at the last minute that he hadn't time to take a
holiday. With Marc, his career came first, and Tessa had
always accepted that. She guessed that Alaric Brent
would be the same type, she rather pitied the girl he
married. Or didn't marry! Cara Everett, her name was,
Freda had said—the company secretary—and good luck
to her. She would need it with a man like Alaric Brent.

She held up the dress on its hanger. Up to now she had never been able to bring herself to wear it. Even looking at it hanging up had reminded her of Marc. But this was the morning when life was beginning again and it was no time to dwell on old miseries. She folded the dress carefully and packed it in her case, with a change of undies and her toilet things. Then, to pass the time until Alaric Brent arrived, she got out her old text-books and immersed herself in them, reminding herself that she was going to be a chemist again and her days as a typist were mercifully over.

The front doorbell rang at ten to one. Tessa looked down through her bedroom window and saw a dark green Jaguar double-parked in front of the house. A thrill of excitement passed through her. This was surely the beginning of something really good.

She glanced in the mirror for a final check, picked up handbag and overnight case and ran down the stairs. This time she was well prepared, she wouldn't react like a zombie when she saw him. He was standing in the hall, wearing casual slacks and an open-neck blue and white striped shirt, and he looked up and smiled as she turned the corner. It was as if her inside suddenly went into spasm and she gripped the banisters and hung on for a few seconds until the feeling passed. It had been easier this time, very soon she would forget all about the resemblance.

She ran down the last few stairs, smiling back at him brilliantly. 'All ready.' She gave him her overnight bag as he held out his hand for it.

'Splendid. It's a grand day—perfect for driving.' He sounded in high good humour today.

Tessa followed Alaric out to the elegant car, which looked slightly out of place in the narrow suburban street of semi-detached villas. He put her case on the back seat and opened the front door for her. As she climbed in she saw old Mrs Rawlings' net curtain being cautiously drawn back. With a mischievous grin Tessa waved through the window as the big car moved smoothly away.

As Alaric had said, it was a perfect day for driving, warm and bright but without too much sun. Tessa sank back into the soft leather seat and sighed with pleasure. After that terrible night of the accident it had been months before she could bring herself to get into a car again, but now, thankfully, she had got over her fear and could actually enjoy driving, so long as she had confidence in the driver. Sometimes, when she went home, she had even nerved herself to drive her father's Ford Escort. She looked at Alaric Brent's strong hands on the wheel and knew intuitively that she was safe with him.

'We won't stop for a meal on the way,' he said. 'I want to get there as soon as possible. We'll pick up a sandwich somewhere and you'll find a bag of grapes in the glove compartment, they'll keep us going.'

The grapes were huge and luscious with hardly any pips. 'My favourite fruit,' Tessa said, selecting one and enjoying the sensuous feeling of the cool juice slipping down her throat.

'Mine too. You'll have to feed the brute, I daren't take my eye off the road just now. Too much traffic.'

He was right, the roads round London were fiendishly busy. Tessa selected a grape and popped it into Alaric's open mouth. He sank his strong teeth into it. 'M'm, lovely! Eve should have fed Adam grapes, not that hard, crunchy apple. More erotic, wouldn't you say? At least they'd have enjoyed themselves before they were cast out of Eden.'

Tessa slid him a guarded glance. This conversation could easily get too intimate. There was something different about Alaric Brent today, something more than merely a change of clothes. Yesterday, in the office, he had been formal, very much the top director appointing a new recruit to his team. Today there was a much easier atmosphere. Well, that was all right with her, it would make the day more pleasant.

'More, please,' he pleaded and opened his mouth again.

Tessa laughed lightly. 'Greedy!' She put another grape into his muth and his teeth caught her finger and bit gently on it.

'Hey, I'm forbidden fruit, I'm warning you.' She pulled her finger away, laughing.

He was laughing too, that low, deep laugh that caught at her memory. 'Thanks for the information. You're a girl who says no, are you?'

'Correct,' said Tessa crisply, and saw that, in spite of the traffic, he slid a quick glance towards her. She kept her eyes resolutely ahead. 'What's our route?' she enquired, changing the subject pointedly. 'I don't suppose you need me to navigate?'

'Oh, no, thanks. I could find my way blindfold,' he said. 'And I could think of much better uses to put you to, Tessa.'

'Like taking a job as chemist in your new lab?'

'We-ell,' he mused. 'Let's say chemistry comes into it.'

Tessa firmed her mouth. 'I'm not sure I like this kind of talk, Mr Brent. It has a touch of sexism about it. Shall we keep our conversation strictly to business?'

'As you wish,' he said mildly. 'Now be a sweet girl and feed me some more grapes.'

So the small sparring match was over. Probably Alaric was bored by the light-hearted exchange. He switched on a tape playing Schubert and concentrated on his driving. He drove fast and well and Tessa sank back into her comfortable seat and admired the skill with which he negotiated the tricky road-switches as the powerful car ate up the miles. Gradually, as they got further west, the traffic thinned out and the landscape became more open. Tessa enjoyed the warmth of the sun on her face and the view of the open road and the rolling grassland and low hills, with here and there small villages and isolated farms. This was somewhere she had never been with Marc; there were no memories to disturb her.

They stopped once, briefly, and bought sandwiches to eat in the car. Then on and on again, mile after mile, until they came into the New Forest. 'Not too far now,' Alaric said. He rolled down the window and took a deep breath. 'This is much better than London, don't you think?'

'Where exactly are we going?' Tessa enquired drowsily. The even purr of the engine, the warmth of the sun, had lulled her almost to sleep. After last night she had a fair amount of sleep to catch up with.

'The nearest town is Wareham—the lab is on the Isle of Purbeck, with the sea on one side and miles of heath on the other. I love it—I hope you will, too, and that it's

not going to be too far from civilisation for you. We'll
have to find somewhere for you to live, of course, and
you'll need a car. You drive?'

'Yes,' said Tessa. He seemed to be taking a good deal
for granted, and she felt herself being swept along on the
tide of his enthusiasm. But even as she found herself
agreeing with everything he said, deep down inside there
was still this lurking fear. Well, not a fear exactly, more
like an uneasiness. Alaric Brent hadn't done or said
anything which might lead her to believe he wanted
more from her than her services in his new laboratory.
He couldn't know how his likeness to Marc added an
odd and disturbing dimension to any relationship they
might have.

She stole a glance at him as he drove. The breeze
through the open window ruffled his dark hair, blowing
it round his ears. He had nice ears, she thought, well
shaped. A little larger than Marc's ears, which had
always seemed small for a man; that was one difference
and she felt quite unreasonably reassured. If she looked
long enough and hard enough she would surely find
others. Not that it really mattered, she told herself
severely, you're going to work for the man, for goodness
sake, not fall in love with him. Just remember that,
Tessa Durant. Remember that next time you fall in
love—if you're ever foolish enough to do so—it will be
with quite a different type of man. Certainly not the
dark and dangerous kind, like Marc—and like Alaric
Brent. She closed her eyes again and drifted away into a
half-sleep.

She wakened when the car stopped and saw that they
were in front of a large, grey stone house whose many

windows twinkled gold in the late afternoon sunshine. There was a bank of trees to the side, and beyond and below the trees she was sure she could hear the sound of the sea.

Alaric was out of the car in a trice; you would never have believed he had been driving for hours, Tessa thought half-admiringly. 'This is it,' he announced with pride as he opened the car door for her. 'Out you get and meet the reception committee. Hello, Barney.' He turned to greet a tall, thin, fair man who was running down the steps towards them.

Alaric said, 'Tessa, this is Barney Grant, our head chemist here. Barney, meet Tessa Durant, who's been hiding her light under a bushel working as a secretary at Head Office, but, as I told you on the phone, she is well qualified to join your team. *If* you can persuade her that living out in the wilds is a rewarding experience.'

The tall man held out a bony hand. 'Hello, Tessa, we'll certainly do our best to convince you.'

Tessa put her hand in his and looked up at him—a long way up. He was one of the tallest men she had met, six feet three or four. In his middle forties, she judged, and with a slight stoop. The eyes behind his gold-rimmed glasses smiled down at her in the nicest possible way and she smiled back, liking him immediately.

'Mona and I are looking forward to putting you up tonight, Miss Durant.' His accent was very faintly Australian.

'Tessa, please. And it's very kind of you.'

'Not a bit of it. It's not so easy to arrange accommodation anywhere near here in the holiday season,' Barney told her as they followed Alaric into the house. 'Do you know this part of the world, Tessa?'

'I don't,' she admitted, 'The Isle of Purbeck isn't really an island, is it?'

'Not really.' He stood aside to let her go through the doorway after Alaric. 'But it's a good spot. It grows on you.'

'You all alone here?' Alaric asked and Barney nodded. 'I hung on, I thought you'd be along soon.'

They were all three inside the house now and Tessa paused, surprised. The big house had obviously been converted from private use into a very businesslike interior. What looked like the original wooden staircase led up from a square hall, in which stood a small reception desk. The walls were wood-panelled with narrow horizontal windows let in all round, above head-level. Several doors led off the hall to right and left and at the far end a passage disappeared into the rear of the house.

Alaric was watching her face. 'This,' he smiled, 'is my new lab. I admit it doesn't look much like one from the outside, but I think you'll agree the builders have done a good job of the conversion.' He looked pleased with himself, as if he had presented a child with a surprise present.

She shook her head puzzledly. 'I suppose I expected a brand-new building, rather like the one in Bristol. But I'm sure it's all splendid,' she added hurriedly, thinking at the same time how absurd it was that she shouldn't want Alaric to believe she was disappointed.

'It is, I assure you,' Barney Grant said. 'We'll show you round later, but first how about going up to your pad for a cuppa, Alaric? Mrs Measures said she'd leave some tea ready before she left, and I'll join you if you'll have me. I've been busy here all day—the men came to instal the new spectrophotometer and they only finished half an hour ago—so I haven't had a chance to get home to eat.'

'It's come? Excellent!' The new equipment was obviously more important to Alaric than Barney's lack of nourishment. 'You take Tessa up while I have a dekko at it.' Without more ado he opened a door on the left and disappeared.

Barney Grant shrugged and made a comic face at Tessa. 'We'd better leave him to it. Come on up, Tessa.' He led the way upstairs.

The first floor had obviously been radically re-vamped also. Tessa saw doors opening into what looked like offices and one door labelled 'Dark Room, Do Not Disturb'. At the end of a passage another door opened into a private suite of rooms.

'This is Alaric's pad,' Barney said. 'He lives on the premises when he's here.' He chuckled. 'Can't drag himself away from the place. Sit down and make yourself comfortable, Tessa, while I brew up the tea.'

'Can't I help?' She followed him into a galley kitchen, fitted with all mod cons including a gleaming microwave cooker and even a built-in dishwasher and washing-machine. Alaric Brent certainly did himself very well. She wondered who worked all these gadgets for him when he was here. Surely he didn't do his own washing? Perhaps one of the girlfriends that Freda Fowkes had mentioned came along to oblige? For some obscure reason the idea rankled in her mind.

Barney switched on the kettle and lifted the white

cloth that covered an oak tea-trolley. Underneath the
cloth were set out blue and white cups and saucers and
plates, a pile of neatly cut sandwiches, crisp scones,
small blue dishes of butter and jam, and on the bottom
shelf an outsized iced walnut cake.

'Great!' The tall man's eyes glistened. 'Mrs Measures
has done us proud. All for Alaric's benefit, of course,
he's Mrs M's hero. Not that she'd admit it, but you can
see her cheeks go pink when Alaric turns up.'

He made the tea and wheeled the trolley into the
living-room next door. Tessa looked round with
approval and slight surprise; it was one of those rooms
that breathed comfort rather than flaunting the slick
modern décor which you might have expected in the
apartment of a top executive. The patterned carpet was
worn in places, the chairs and sofas were outsized and
furnished with plump, inviting chintz-covered cushions.
An old roll-top desk stood against one wall and an oak
gate-leg table in a corner of the room. The velvet
curtains were pale pink and streaked paler by the sun.
Perhaps Alaric had been too busy with the lab to get
around to furnishing his apartment to match his image
as a director of Brent's.

Tessa sank into one of the deep chairs with a sigh of
pleasure.

'Tired?' Barney enquired. 'Or did Alaric's driving
reduce you to a nervous wreck—he's a devil when he
gets behind the wheel of a car.'

'Rubbish,' came a voice from the doorway, and Alaric
walked into the room. 'My driving is faultless.' He took
a chair opposite Tessa and his dark eyes held hers as he
added deliberately, 'I reserve the devilish side of my

character for more rewarding pursuits.'

She felt a small twinge inside as she recognised that look; she had seen it before, in Marc's eyes, when they first met. Alaric Brent was a dark and dangerous man too, the kind she had promised herself to avoid, but already she felt the pull of his masculinity.

She reminded herself that after today she wouldn't be seeing much of him. Already she was fascinated by what she had seen of the countryside here. Already she was lured by the interest of the job Alaric offered. She just had to be very careful to avoid anything personal between them, that was all.

After tea they inspected the lab. Down here Alaric was in his element, showing off his new 'baby' as he had called it, and again Tessa felt his enthusiasm rubbing off on to her. It was just the kind of place she would love to work in: everything spick and span and new. The white walls with their rows of built-in cupboards; all the usual laboratory equipment—stands of test-tubes and beakers and retorts, their glass gleaming and ready for the labels that would appear when work really started. Spotless sinks, cabinets with banks of shallow drawers.

There were larger items too. 'This is the latest counter-current distributor,' Alaric announced, touching a complex net of tubes lovingly. 'And this is the spectrophotometer, which double-checks the final vital ingredients when they've been extracted and purified. That's right, isn't it, Barney?'

The tall chemist nodded. 'It's a bit like panning for gold,' he explained. 'The plant's raw substances are cleaned and dissolved away until only the tiniest spot of pure extract remains. And that contains perhaps a chemical or crystal never before tested medically. And after all the tests, if it proves harmful or not effective, it's discarded and we start all over again with another plant.'

The three of them were walking around the lab, between the benches, and once when they paused to lean over some new bit of equipment, Tessa's breast brushed against Alaric's arm. She could feel the hard muscle solid and strong against her own softness and her heart started to thump wildly against her ribs. She moved away quickly but she knew that he, too, had registered the contact.

The indecision of yesterday returned. It was stupid and illogical but she had the strongest presentiment that she was running into danger. Perhaps, even at the risk of losing a marvellous job, she should have nothing to do with this man. Perhaps she should tell him so now, this minute. Perhaps it would be sane and wise to say, 'It's all marvellously impressive and I'm sure you'll do some splendid work here but before we go any further I've got to tell you the truth. I wouldn't want to live here, I'm afraid. It's too remote for me.'

But she didn't say it and Alaric was away again, on his pet topic. 'We've done some preliminary work on a plant that grows in South America—we call it FB23—and as I told you it seems to hold a good deal of promise.'

From a cubicle at the end of the lab a telephone burred. Barney went to answer it and Alaric halted, looking towards him, waiting for a message perhaps.

When Barney rejoined them his face was white. 'It was the hospital. My wife—Mona—she's been rushed in.' He ran his fingers through his hair in a distraught gesture. 'The baby wasn't due for another month. I'll have to go to her.'

'Of course you will,' Alaric said immediately. 'What can I do to help?'

Barney shook his head as if he could clear his mind. 'If you could give me a lift—you see, I left the car at home for Mona to shop. She was going to pick me up here when I phoned and——'

Already Alaric was leading the way from the lab and out of the building towards the green Jaguar standing on the gravel sweep in front. 'You lock up, Barney,' he said over his shoulder. 'We'll have you to the hospital in no time.' Barney was fumbling with his keys and locking the doors behind him as he left.

Tessa climbed into the back seat of the car, not saying anything because Barney wouldn't want any intrusion into his worry from a stranger. As the car turned and speeded away along the lanes she felt empty inside, praying that this nice man's nice wife—she must be nice—wasn't going to lose her baby, remembering with horrible clarity the dull, empty hopelessness that had come down on her like a thick fog a year ago.

At the hospital Alaric said, 'We'll wait, old chap, until you find out what's going on.'

'Thanks.' Barney's eyes were roaming everywhere, at the rows of leather-covered seats, at the woman behind the reception desk, at the couple of white-coated young doctors who strolled past talking. Finally he tackled the two doctors. They spoke for a moment and then one of them nodded and led Barney away.

'We may as well sit down,' Alaric said. 'I suppose we may have quite a wait.'

There were only two people waiting there besides themselves—an elderly woman and a youngish man—and they looked as if they had been there some time. Things move slowly in hospitals, as Tessa well remembered, except in cases of emergency. She remembered her own emergency, all those months ago. Her mother's face looking down at her, smiling bravely through her tears, holding her hand, saying she was going to get better and everything would come right. But it hadn't come right, of course. Her injuries healed in time, but there wasn't going to be any baby. Or any Marc either.

'Poor old Barney—a bit of a shock for him. It's their first,' Alaric said, breaking into her sombre thoughts. 'They're the most delightful couple.'

'Um?' She looked dazedly at him. 'Oh, yes.' She pulled herself together. 'I liked Barney very much.'

'He's a rare bird—brilliant at his job, straightforward, absolutely dependable. They don't come like that too often these days. You'll enjoy working with him.'

Here it was again—he was taking it for granted that she was going to accept the job. But this seemed the wrong moment to take a stand about refusing it, so she missed her chance again and sat there saying nothing and feeling angry with herself because she was much too aware of Alaric's thigh touching hers as they sat on the rather narrow chairs.

They were silent after that and with every moment that passed she got the feeling that she was caught in a situation that was getting more and more difficult to get out of. Alaric stretched out his long legs in front of him and Tessa took the opportunity of moving sideways so that their bodies didn't touch. His head turned slightly and she knew that he had noticed, but she didn't dare to meet his eyes.

He shifted in his seat. 'These chairs,' he growled, 'are going to get harder and harder the longer we sit here. I think I'll make a nuisance of myself and go and see if I can find out what's happening.'

He walked across the entrance hall and the grey-haired woman behind the reception desk leaned forward and eyed him in an affronted kind of way as he disappeared from sight in the direction that the young doctor had taken Barney.

He was away for some time and when he came back he bent towards Tessa to speak in a low voice. 'I saw Barney. He's staying with his wife and he'll probably be here all night.'

Tessa stood up. 'Is she—has the baby been born?'

He shook his head. 'No, they're hoping to delay it for a week or so but they seem to be reasonably satisfied with Mona's condition. There's nothing we can do at present. Barney's upset about having to let you down about the plans to give you a meal and a bed for the night but I told him I'd look after you. There's one thing we must do first. Mona was apparently preparing supper for us when the pains started. She got in a bit of a state and all she managed to do was stagger to the phone and dial 999 and call an ambulance. Now she's worrying in case she left things switched on in her kitchen. Barney's given me a spare key and I said we'd look in and make sure that everything was OK. So we'll get along there straight away.'

It was almost dark by now as they drove back the way

they had come from the laboratory. Eventually the car pulled up in front of a row of four cottages. None of them had lights in the windows and the front gardens looked untended. 'The Grants only moved in last week,' Alaric said over his shoulder as he opened the door of the end cottage and switched on a light. 'They were just getting straight.'

'Something's burning,' Tessa gasped and looked round for the door into the kitchen. A faint brown haze was issuing from the electric cooker and she reached out to open the oven-door but Alaric grabbed her arm. 'Steady on, let me do it.' He wrapped a cloth round the handle before he opened the door to disclose a charred black mess in a pyrex pie-dish. On the hob a pan which had probably once contained potatoes was even blacker. 'Our supper,' he said wryly, switching off everything on the cooker. 'Poor old Mona, a wasted effort.'

He sounded quite upset about it. Could he be that rare animal, Tessa wondered, a man who actually considered other people's feelings? Was she being unfair when she had been so ready to believe he was like Marc, just because he looked like him?

'I'll clear up the place a bit,' Alaric said, transferring everything gingerly to the sink and trickling cold water in so that a loud hissing noise ensued. 'We can't let old Barney come home to this, on top of everything else.' He examined the dish and the pan and tried to scrape out the contents. After a few moments of fruitless effort he turned, knife in hand, raising dark eyebrows. 'What do you think? Hopeless?'

'Hopeless,' Tessa said sadly.

'Dustbin?'

'I'm afraid so.'

Together they located the dustbin outside the back
door and dumped the pathetic remains of the supper in
it. Then they returned to the kitchen and Alaric cleaned
the cooker while Tessa dealt with the sink and the
draining-board. There was an odd comradeship about it
all. If the circumstances hadn't been as they were it
might easily have been fun. But as it was they didn't talk
at all, and when the job was done Alaric locked the back
door again and they went out into the hall.

'What now?' he said. 'We'd better think about supper,
I'm starving, are you, Tessa? Afternoon tea is delightful
but I need something much more solid inside me now. I
can't think of anywhere near where we'd get a decent
meal this late. We'll go back to my apartment and raid
the freezer.'

There wouldn't be anyone else in the whole building
now, and Tessa felt distinctly uneasy about the prospect
of being alone with Alaric there. But already he had
locked the cottage door and was half-way down the path
towards the Jaguar. 'Tomorrow morning,' he said, 'we'll
come over here and you can drive Barney's car to the
hospital, so that he won't be stuck without transport.
OK? It's a Ford Escort. You can manage that?'

'Oh yes,' she said. 'My father's car's an Escort, I
sometimes drive it when I go home.' She had driven
only two or three times since the accident, a year ago,
but she wasn't going to tell him that.

'Good. Hop in, then, and we'll have a meal going in
no time.'

Tessa hesitated. 'But—the plan was for me to stay the
night here with Barry and his wife. I could easily find

the spare room, I'm sure.'

He opened the car door for her. In the faint light she could see his teeth flash white in a smile. 'A girl has to know where she's going to sleep, is that it?'

'That's exactly it,' said Tessa firmly.

'Well, there's one place where you're certainly *not* going to sleep and that's here. Do you think I'd leave you alone in the middle of nowhere? None of the other cottages are occupied at present.' He took her arm, urging her towards the car.

But she stood her ground, although the pressure of his hand was sending the blood rushing up into her face. It was a good thing it was too dark for him to see it. 'You wouldn't be changing the subject, would you?' she enquired.

He laughed aloud. 'What a suspicious young woman you are, Tessa Durant. No, I'll do some ringing around and find a room for you. You must imagine I'm really crass to start something with you at this early stage of our acquaintance.'

'I don't think you're crass, Mr Brent,' Tessa said. 'All I know is that you're masculine.'

He was still laughing. 'I can't deny it. I can only promise that you're perfectly safe with me, Tessa. And for God's sake don't call me Mr Brent. I'm not the big boss up here, we're colleagues. Come along, get in and we'll argue the toss about where you're going to sleep later on.'

Reluctantly she got into the car and he slammed the door. He needn't, she thought, have been quite so amused at the idea that he might fancy her. Not that she wanted him to, of course, the very opposite was the case.

And anyway, she wondered if he was telling the truth. She might just have been imagining it, but she had the feeling that several signals had come from him that hadn't been strictly connected with business.

But she wasn't going to make a fool of herself by acting like an inexperienced teenager. She argued with herself that she was perfectly capable of handling any situation that might crop up, she wasn't afraid of Alaric Brent. She knew, deep down, that it was herself she was afraid of. Because this was the way it had started with Marc, she recognised the vulnerability in herself, recognised the immediate body chemistry between them. Just a look, a touch was enough. And she didn't intend to lay herself open to suffering like that ever again.

When she fell in love again—*if* she ever fell in love again—it would be with a man different from Marc in every possible way. She tried to picture him as the big car drove through the darkening lanes. He would have fair, rumpled hair, and crinkles beside his eyes, and he would love children and animals and he wouldn't be a high-flyer like Marc—like Alaric Brent. He would enjoy his job but he wouldn't be over-ambitious. And he would be kind and thoughtful and—Tessa sighed as the car came to a halt. It seemed unlikely that such a paragon would exist.

And even more unlikely that she would fall in love with him if he did.

CHAPTER THREE

IT WAS almost dark by now. In the lights from the car the old house loomed grey and solid against its backdrop of pines, and when the car engine stopped the quietness closed round them. There was only the soughing of the sea far below and the distant bleat of a sheep who had missed her bedtime. Their footsteps echoed on the wooden stairs and when Alaric opened the door of his apartment and switched off the lights on the ground floor below there seemed to be a great well of darkness down there. Tessa thought that she wouldn't like to stay here alone, as he did. But he wouldn't be on his own, of course. There would be Cara Everett, or if not her some other hopeful female. Men like Alaric Brent would never need to spend their nights alone.

'Food first,' he said, striding into the kitchen. Tessa followed and leaned against the breakfast-bar, watching his broad back as he rummaged in the freezer, tossing packages to right and left. In spite of herself her eyes fixed themselves on his lean hips and strong taut thighs straining against the well fitting tightness of his trousers, and a stirring in the region of her stomach made her catch her breath.

'Found anything exciting?' she said lightly.

He turned from the freezer and their eyes met

across the kitchen, and her words hung in the air
between them.

Then, 'Yes,' he said softly. 'I rather think I have.'

She couldn't look away. She waited, lips parted, for
what would happen next. But Alaric turned back to
the freezer and pulled out a packet, knocked off its
loose covering of snow into the sink, and read,
'Halibut in Mornay Sauce. How does that appeal?'

'Sounds delicious,' she said in a tight, social voice.

He pulled more packages out and read the labels.
'With *petits pois* and Duchesse potatoes. Yes?'

'Lovely!' He sounded so ordinary that she relaxed a
little and realised that she was hungry. She had been
too excited to eat much breakfast, and grapes and a
sandwich on the journey, followed by a slice of walnut
cake at teatime, didn't really add up to enough to keep
a healthy young woman's appetite satisfied. 'What can
I do to help?'

'Nothing yet. We'll follow the instructions on the
packets and then get ourselves a drink while the
marvels of modern sience are doing their stuff.' He
gestured towards the microwave cooker.

In the sitting-room she sat in the corner of the sofa
and sipped her drink. Alaric switched on the electric
fire in the big open grate with the marble surround
and stood with his back to it. 'Even in June it can be
chilly in these parts when the wind's blowing off the
sea,' he said, but he said it with a kind of relish.

'You enjoy it here?' she asked politely, keeping the
conversation at the social-chat level.

'Love it. It's part of my childhood.' He came and sat
beside her on the sofa. 'I spent most of my school

holidays here with my grandparents. My mama was always too busy with her work as chairman of the company to bother with having me at home.' He paused for a moment, grey eyes thoughtful. 'My grandfather died a couple of years ago—just a year after my grandmother—and he left me this house in his will. Somehow making it into my own lab seemed to be a kind of memorial. I couldn't bear to part with it and it's much too large to keep as a hideaway for weekends. My mama wasn't too keen on the idea of the lab but there wasn't much she could do about it. I own a share of the company.'

'Your mother's been head of the company for a long time?' Tessa knew that Mrs Brent was chairman, but she had never actually seen her. The opinion on the grapevine was that she was a formidable lady.

'A very long time. Ever since my father died when I was eight. It was a much smaller set-up then than it is now, we've bought up several subsidiary companies. Mama's made a wonderful job of it, a real success story. I admire her more than I can say, she's an excellent businesswoman.'

'I'm sure she is,' said Tessa politely, and was glad that her mother wasn't chairman of a great company. No wonder Alaric had adored his grandparents.

She broke the silence. 'Shouldn't you be ringing around to find me a room for the night?'

He turned to her, raising one dark eyebrow. 'If you insist.'

'I do,' she said. He was making a joke of this, but it might turn out to be anything but a joke.

He went across to the desk and pulled the telephone

towards him and dialled. 'Woolpack Inn? A single room for tonight? No? OK, thank you.'

Five minutes and four more hotels later he replaced the receiver and came back to the sofa, lowering his long body down beside her. 'Sorry about that,' he said, but he didn't sound particularly sorry. 'It's the tourist season, you see.'

Tessa pursed her lips. 'You knew this would happen, didn't you? Well, what now?'

He grinned. 'I like you when you look fierce. It's quite a change to see a girl jealously guarding what she considers her honour. I'm afraid you'll have to accept my hospitality here. There's only one bed and I sense that you might snarl at me if I suggested that we share it. So I'll be a perfect gent and sleep on the sofa here. It's very comfy.' He pressed down the soft cushions.

'And please don't look like that, Tessa,' he went on. 'I brought you here, it's my responsibility. I wasn't planning a seduction, if that's what you're thinking, and I'm certainly not going to take advantage of the fact that Mona has been whisked away to hospital. You must admit that I couldn't have arranged that.'

Reluctantly her lips drew into an answering smile. 'I've just got a suspicious nature, I suppose.'

'And you're a lady who says no, aren't you?' He was joking again by referring to their conversation in the car.

'Right,' she said crisply, pretending not to have noticed.

'Ah well,' he sighed in mock disappointment. 'It's better to know where we stand.' He stood up. 'Now let's go and see if our supper's ready.' He held out his hands in a friendly way to pull her to her feet and it would have been churlish to ignore the gesture.

She put her hands in his but when she was standing before him he didn't release them. Holding both hands he looked seriously down into her face and said quietly. 'I'm no callow youth, Tessa. I can control myself. You haven't anything to fear from me.'

His fingers closed round hers and his grip was firm and warm. She could feel the warmth all through her body. She released her hands and walked in front of him into the kitchen. That way he couldn't see the colour that flooded into her cheeks. It's not you I'm afraid of, she thought in dismay, it's myself. Oh, why did I get into this? I should never, never have agreed to come.

Alaric was quite evidently setting himself out to reassure her. Supper was a friendly meal, free from personal innuendoes. He did most of the talking. At first he concentrated on his new lab and his plans for it, but as he refilled their wine glasses, and the halibut was followed by lychees and then by biscuits and cheese, he told her about his boyhood here in this old house with his grandparents.

'I loved coming here in the school holidays. My grandparents used to give me the spoiling I never got at home. After my father died, I suppose my mama was too busy to do much spoiling. My sister was ten years older and beyond the spoiling stage. But my grandmother made up for it. I remember she used to make the most wonderful bread-and-butter pudding. All golden and crusty on the top with black chewy raisins sticking up out of it. Yummy!' He licked his lips, and Tessa smiled, seeing him as a greedy schoolboy. It seemed to make him less of a threat to her peace of mind.

He went over to a carved oak cupboard and took out a bottle of brandy and two glasses. He patted the cupboard lovingly, adding, 'All the furniture belonged to the original house. I couldn't bear to put new modern stuff in.'

'I like it,' Tessa said, sipping the tiny amount of brandy he had poured into her glass. 'It looks at home here.'

He nodded. 'I'm afraid I get sentimental about my youth when I come here. My grandfather was a splendid old boy. We used to walk for miles, sometimes over the heath, sometimes along the lanes and up into the hills. He told me stories about old Purbeck—about the grisly history of the place and what they did with the pirates when they caught them. He had an old boat and sometimes we'd sail round the coast and watch the cormorants and he'd point out all the different strata in the rocks. Purbeck's a geologist's paradise—if you walk from Studland Beach to Chapman's Pool you pass over two hundred million years of rock history. There were lots of dinosaurs in these parts, you know. They left fossil traces all over the place.'

Tessa was watching his face. The straight mouth had softened; he was caught up in something that fascinated him. She thought he had a rather rare gift of enthusing about things outside himself. She remembered how Marc had only liked talking about himself and his career. But perhaps that was partly her fault; she had encouraged him and indulged him, she knew that now.

Alaric turned to her, grinning wryly. 'Sorry, I must be boring you. Talking about places isn't nearly as good as seeing them. I must take you round some of my favourite spots.'

Tessa lowered her head over her plate and made no reply. Was he intentionally linking them together or was this just social chat, rather like, 'You must come and have a meal with us'—that polite promise made so often and just as often forgotten?

'That was lovely,' she said as they cleared the plates on to the trolley and Alaric wheeled it into the kitchen. 'Convenience foods for ever!'

He switched on the coffee-machine. 'I second that. They make it possible for a mere man to look after himself.'

'From choice of course.' Tessa laughed, stacking the plates in the dishwasher.

'Oh, certainly. I've always been too busy to settle down and I doubt if I'm a domestic animal.'

So—they had both declared their position. As he had said a little while ago, it was as well to know where they stood.

Tessa carried the coffee tray back into the living-room. With the curtains drawn against the darkness outside, and the glow of the fire on the well-worn carpet and the chintzy covers of the sofa and chairs, it looked warm and comfortable.

Alaric put the coffee tray on a low table beside the sofa. 'Now wasn't I right?' he said. 'This is much to be preferred to spending the night alone in that empty cottage.'

'I wouldn't have done it from choice,' Tessa admitted. 'The cottages looked rather lonely, being unoccupied, and I'm not very brave. I would have been imagining spiders and mice.'

Alaric leaned forward to pour out the coffee. 'We'll have all the livestock removed before you take up residence. The other two cottages are already spoken for, but the one next to the Grants can be yours.'

'What *is* this?' She made her voice light. 'Am I being—what's the word—press-ganged? I haven't said I'm coming to work here yet.'

'But you will, won't you? I want you to come.' There was more than a touch of arrogance in his voice.

Their eyes met across the width of the sofa and the silence became charged as if hundreds of volts of electricity were passing between them.

Tessa said as coolly as she could manage, 'And do you always get what you want, Mr——'

'Alaric.'

'All right then, Alaric. Do you?'

'I don't recognise the word failure,' he said, and his eyes didn't move from hers. Her mouth was dry and she couldn't say a word. Neither could she look away from him. The smoky-grey eyes held hers effortlessly.

He said quietly, 'You know, ever since that interview yesterday when you were so jittery and you couldn't look at me, I haven't been able to get you out of my mind. I wanted to know why you behaved as you did. You intrigued me. Tell me about that other chap.'

Her green eyes widened. 'What do you mean? What other chap?'

'My dear girl! One doesn't need to be a psychiatrist to see that some fellow has hurt you pretty badly. I'd like to prove to you that not all men are heels.'

She shook her head vehemently. 'You're wasting your time,' she said. 'I'm still a girl who says no.'

He returned to his corner of the sofa, sitting back and surveying her lazily. 'You mean—you really intend to hold out for marriage? A girl with a passionate nature like yours?'

Tessa's eyes flashed green fire. 'You don't know a thing about my nature, and "holding out for marriage" was the way *you* put it. I find the term insulting. As if I were out to get a husband at any price and was prepared to descend to trickery to do it. Like most girls I want marriage—eventually—but a good marriage with a man who doesn't just want to get me into bed and can't get me any other way.'

'H'm.' He seemed to be considering that. 'What happened, Tessa?' he asked quietly.

Her head jerked round so quickly that her dark silky hair slapped against her cheek. 'What do you mean, what happened?'

He shrugged. 'It's obvious that something happened to account for your defensiveness. I said you were a passionate girl and I meant it—a man can tell, you know, you can't hide it. Do you really mean to keep yourself in purdah until Mr Right comes along to offer you his name and endow you with all his worldly goods?'

'I'm not fussy about worldly goods,' Tessa said coldly, 'but—yes—I want a certain security.'

'Ah—security.' He shook his head, smiling grimly. 'Security doesn't exist in this world. Only people exist, flesh and blood people. You have to take them on trust.'

'Trust!' She couldn't keep the bitterness from her voice.

'Ah!' he breathed softly again. He leaned towards the table. 'You've let your coffee go cold. Give me your cup and I'll pour it away and give you some more.' He departed towards the kitchen with her half-full cup of cold coffee.

She watched him go, a small frown settling between her eyes. It was impossible to believe that she had known him for only a couple of days. Everything about him was so familiar—he even walked like Marc, with a long, relaxed stride, his dark head held easily on his broad shoulders. But Marc wouldn't have noticed that her coffee had gone cold. And if he had he certainly wouldn't have gone to the trouble of getting her a fresh cup.

She shook her head impatiently. It was stupid to go on comparing the two men like this, she must stop it. It wasn't as if there were likely to be an intimate relationship between Alaric Brent and herself, she was determined that there wouldn't be, whatever he had in mind himself.

But perhaps they could meet on a friendly basis if she took the job here. He wouldn't be here very often, he had told her that. Friends and colleagues. Yes, she would like that.

Alaric returned with her cup and this time he sat himself down close to her on the red velvet sofa. So close that his arm rested against hers as he leaned forward to fill her cup. His head was lowered and she could smell the subtle masculine smell of his skin and a faint whiff of some cologne mingled with it. She had a wild urge to rub her cheek against his hair. What was she thinking of? She must be mad.

'Thank you,' she murmured, taking a long drink. Now that Alaric had poured her coffee he might have been expected to move back again to his original position, but instead he stayed where he was, much too close to her, stretching his long legs in front of him and resting an arm along the back of the sofa.

'I always feel happy here,' he said dreamily, 'as if nice things were just round the corner. A throwback from childhood, I expect. When you come to think of it, our lives are made up of our memories, they're us. We have to accept them as part of ourselves, but we mustn't let the past rule the present—or the future.'

'Deep stuff,' Tessa smiled. Keep it light, my girl, whatever you do. 'I rather suspect that little lecture was aimed at me.'

'Clever girl.' He lowered his hand from the back of the sofa and rested it on her neck. She shivered and moved her head away as the touch of his fingers, strong and yet gentle, made her stomach jolt.

'Please don't,' she whispered.

'Why not?' His voice was deep, close to her ear. 'Why not, Tessa? You can't lock yourself up with your memories whatever they are. You can't live in the past.'

His grip tightened on her neck and he turned her head so that their faces were only inches apart. Her eyes focused themselves on his mouth. It had been so long since she yearned for a man's kisses, but now——

'You're so lovely,' he breathed huskily. 'So damnably desirable.' His mouth buried itself in the warm curve of her neck.

So damnably desirable—Marc had said that on the first night they made love and she had thrilled to the words, feeling herself a woman, an attractive woman, desired by this wonderful man, longing to give him every little bit of her, to satisfy his need. What a stupid fool she had been!

'No!' The word exploded with violence from her. She pushed Alaric away. 'I won't—I told you——'

She drew in a deep, shaky breath. Perhaps the saying that history repeated itself was true. She had determined to get as far away from the past as she could, and now it seemed that fate was dragging her back into it. First the offer of the job—now this! Escape seemed the only way.

She got up and stood with her back to him and although her voice was not quite steady her resolve came through firmly enough. 'I'm sorry if I gave you the wrong impression when I agreed to come here with you. I think it would be sensible if I said no again—to the job, I mean. That is, if you intend to offer it to me.'

'Tessa, I didn't——' he began.

Then, without warning, the only light in the room—from the standard lamp in the corner—went out, and the red glow of the fire began quickly to fade.

Alaric swore colourfully. 'The blasted generator's gone on the blink again. We have to rely on it until they've finished working on the electrics in the lab. I'll have to go down and see what's wrong.'

Tessa dragged herself back into the everyday world where generators could go wrong. 'Can I do anything?' she offered absurdly—what did she know about generators?

In the darkness she felt his hand close over hers. 'You just stay put, darling,' he said. 'I won't be long.'

She saw the thin beam of a pencil torch, which he evidently kept in his pocket. The light moved across the room; she heard the door open and Alaric's footsteps on the wooden stairs. Then she was alone in the dark.

It was cold now the fire had gone out. She wrapped her arms round herself and waited, it seemed for ages. There was only one thought in her mind—he had called her 'darling'. It had come out so naturally, as if they had known each other for years. As if they were already lovers.

I'm in danger of falling in love with him, she thought. I've got to stop it before it's too late. It was all happening just as it had happened before when she first met Marc. She recognised the wild tumult of her senses that had made her lose her power of reasoning once, but it mustn't happen again.

Her eyes were growing accustomed to the dark now. A faint light showed round the edges of the curtains and she moved across the room cautiously and pulled them back. There was no moon, no stars even, only the dim afterglow of the sunset, streaks of silver-grey

and apricot against the thick bank of clouds. Tessa
shivered. What was Alaric doing down there? He
seemed to have been gone for ages. What did you have
to do to make a generator work, she wondered
vaguely. Was it a specialist job—was there danger
involved? Electric shock? She had a horrifying picture
of Alaric lying down there somewhere, sense-
less—perhaps—perhaps——

Her teeth were chattering as she stumbled across
the room to the open door. Feeling her way along the
wall of the corridor she came out on to the landing
where a faint light from the long window showed her
the top of the stairway. Down to the ground floor and
into the entrance hall. Here there were no windows
but Alaric had left the front door open. She stumbled
down the three outside steps and along a path that
seemed to lead round the side of the house. The
generator would be in an outbuilding somewhere. Out
of doors it was easier to make out the shape of things,
the tall pine trees, the rough stone wall of the house,
the faint glint of windows. She turned the corner and
saw the dark shape of a barn, or an outhouse of some
sort. A likely place for an electric generator.

'Alaric!' she called. 'Hi, Alaric—are you there?'

'Here!' His voice came to her, muffled, urgent.
'Tessa—can you come?'

Something was horribly wrong, she knew it. Her
heart was in her mouth as she stumbled over the damp
ground towards the shadowy, bulky shape of the barn.
'Where are you—I can't see very much.'

'Over here—by the door. I dropped the bloody
torch—can you find it?' The words seemed to be

forced between clenched teeth.

As Tessa moved cautiously forward her shoe kicked something that made a metallic sound. The torch! Mercifully it still worked. In its tiny circle of light she saw that Alaric was on his back, supported on his elbows. A jumble of massively thick logs of wood were lying across his legs, just above the ankle, pinning him down.

For a moment Tessa felt faint; then the moment passed. She had done a first-aid course years ago, in the sixth form at school, and she knew about shock. 'What happened, can you tell me what to do?' She kept her voice calm.

'I can't—move.' The words came out raggedly.

'Keep still and let me look.'

The logs looked terrifyingly thick and heavy. She bit her lip hard. If she tried to lift them and failed they might fall back and do some horrible damage. But in all probability horrible damage was already being done. She pushed down a feeling of nausea.

She propped the torch up against the step of the barn. 'There are three logs holding you down,' she said as calmly as she could. 'I'm going to lift them. Are you ready?'

'Yes,' he groaned. 'Hurry, for God's sake.'

Praying under her breath she grasped one end of the top log and heaved it upwards and sideways. It fell clear.

'Now for number two,' she muttered. The second log was thicker and heavier. Her shoulder muscles trembled as they took the strain but she held on and at last the log joined the first one.

For a moment or two she rested, breathing hard, gathering her strength. Then, 'Only one left now,' she said, and heaven only knew how she kept her voice cheerful.

It was the thickest and heaviest of them all, the trunk of a forest tree, and one of Alaric's legs was held firmly beneath it; the other leg had been freed now, but she could see that it would have been impossible for him to lift the final log himself from the position he was lying in.

'Here we go then.' She put both hands under the log, bent her knees, and heaved upwards against the dead weight, her teeth digging into her lower lip. Her shoulders were on fire, her wrists seemed to be cracking. The sweat was pouring down her face. For one horrendous moment she felt her whole body giving way under the strain. Then, sobbing as she heaved, she felt the log move.

'I can't—lift it—any further,' she forced the words through clenched teeth. 'Can you pull your foot out backwards?'

She could hear his harsh breathing. She strained to hold the weight, her eyes fixed on the beam of light that showed her how far the log was above Alaric's leg. It seemed hardly to have lifted at all. Her arms were being wrenched from her body. The rough bark was cutting into her hands. Oh God, she couldn't hold it any longer. Then she saw Alaric's foot begin to move, inch by painful inch, as he levered himself on his elbows, dragging himself backwards.

'That's it,' she cried at last. 'You're free. Oh, thank God, thank God.' The log of wood fell to the ground with a thud and Tessa collapsed beside it and lay speechless, hardly conscious.

Presently she roused herself and in the light of the torch she saw the outline of Alaric's body, lying close beside her, frighteningly still. 'Alaric——' She put out her arm to touch him and winced at the pain in her shoulder. 'Alaric,' she babbled, 'Alaric—say something—are you—are you——'

'Alive?' came Alaric's deep voice, and it was almost steady. 'I think so. I never thought I'd—end up—at the bottom of a pile of pik-a-stiks. You remember that old kids' game?'

Tessa fought back hysterical laughter. 'Are you hurt? How bad is it?'

He pulled himself into a sitting position and moved his hands down his legs. 'I think I've been lucky—nothing broken as far as I can tell. The ground's soft—that must have saved me—that, and you, Tessa. You've been bloody marvellous.'

'Girl Guide, that's me.' She was feeling a little intoxicated with success. He was safe and she had helped to save him.

She wriggled her shoulders and give a little gasp. His hand reached out and touched her arm. 'My poor child, what have you done to yourself?'

She gulped. 'Nothing much. Nothing that a hot bath won't put right.' He edged closer to her and she felt the comforting warmth of his body through her thin blouse. She laid her head against his shoulder and fought back the tears.

'Such a little thing,' he murmured. 'I really don't know how you managed.'

'Not so little,' she giggled weakly. 'But it might have been easier if I'd been a couple of stone heavier, to qualify as a weight-lifter.'

'God forbid,' Alaric said fervently. 'Now then, what's to be done? I'm afraid there's no hope of dealing with the generator tonight, but look, our luck's in. The moon's coming up.'

It wasn't a full moon, but its silver light shone brilliantly against the deep blackness of the sky, outshining the stars. The light was sufficient to illuminate them and their surroundings. Tessa saw the pile of massive logs, as they had fallen, and shuddered. Alaric turned his head towards them. 'The contractors have been cutting down some trees. God!' he burst out in disgust. 'When I find out who's responsible for propping this lot up against the barn instead of making them into a neat pile on the ground I'll have his scalp. But never mind about that now, we must get ourselves up to the apartment. Can you walk OK?'

Tessa got to her feet. 'Of course. But can you?'

'We'll see.'

She had to turn her head away so that she couldn't see his face as he struggled to his feet, cursing under his breath. But at last he was standing. 'There's a short branch over there,' he said. 'If you could give me that and if I could rest my other hand on your shoulder, Tessa, I think I can manage. I'll try not to lean too heavily.'

It was painfully slow going but at last they reached the front door. 'From here on I'm a toddler again,' Alaric announced and she wondered what it cost him to laugh as he sat down and ascended the stairs backwards, bumping on to each stair and easing his legs behind him. Then he was on his feet again, shuffling along the corridor and into the living-room of the apartment.

He sank on to the sofa and let out a long breath. 'Well, here we are, that's the biggest hurdle crossed.' He paused. 'What do you feel about ringing for an ambulance and both of us being carted off to hospital?'

'Oh, no,' Tessa gasped impulsively. Then, 'But perhaps you ought to.'

He said, 'Evidently you don't like hospitals any more than I do, and I doubt if it's really necessary in my case. I'm sure I'll be black and blue in the morning but I'm equally sure it's nothing worse. I dare say I'm being foolhardy but what I suggest is that we have a night's sleep and then we can assess the damage in the daylight. Do you agree?'

'Oh, yes,' Tessa said fervently. She had good reason to be grateful to hospitals—or rather, to the staff who had saved her life—and she was grateful, but no, not again, not tonight.

'Come here, close to me,' Alaric said. 'Down on the floor, where I can reach you. Now, tell me where your shoulders hurt.'

He probed gently, his fingers sensitive to her reactions. She winced one or twice but only in one spot on her left shoulder was there any real pain, and that was a dull pain, not acute. 'You see,' she said, 'it's only a muscular strain, nothing serious.'

'I hope so, indeed I do.' He had finished probing

and his arm drew her close as she knelt on the carpet before him. 'I'd never forgive myself if I'd really harmed you.' He leaned over and planted a kiss on the top of her head. 'Your hair's like black satin in the moonlight,' he added softly, and she lifted her face, surprised.

His mouth came down on hers in a long, quiet kiss, and Tessa yielded herself to the warm delight that enveloped her. Her lips clung to his and she wanted the kiss to go on and on.

'That's by way of saying thank you. Now, do you think you could go on being Florence Nightingale and pour me a spot of brandy. I—need it rather badly just now.' She heard him stifle a groan. 'I'd get it myself but my legs are somewhat non-functional just at the moment.'

The room was getting lighter as the moon rose higher in the sky and its white light shone directly through the window. Tessa found the drinks cupboard and poured a large brandy at Alaric's direction.

'And one for yourself,' he told her and she obeyed that command too. Reaction was beginning to set in and she felt cold and shaky.

The brandy slid down her throat, warming and reviving. 'Now,' she said, taking charge of the situation, 'we must have a look at the damage to your legs, and if there is an open wound then I'm sure you should get advice.'

He sighed. 'Maybe you're right. I can't afford to be stupid about it.' She saw the way his mouth twisted as he added, 'I'm afraid I'll have to ask you to help to get my trousers off.'

'No problem,' Tessa said firmly. 'Florence Nightingale wouldn't have balked at a little job like that.'

He chuckled. 'You really are rather special, little Tessa. OK, go ahead.' He pulled down the zip.

Very carefully she lifted both his legs on to the sofa and removed his shoes. Then she eased off the trousers as gently as she could while he helped her by lifting himself on his hands.

'That's it,' she said. 'Now, let's look at the damage.'

He sat up and examined both his legs by the light of the torch while Tessa watched, biting her lip, not knowing what to expect. But at last he leaned back with a grunt of satisfaction. 'As I thought. Nothing broken, not even the skin—it's a let-off. As for the bruising—I'll have to get that vetted tomorrow, but there's no immediate urgency.'

'Are you *sure?*' Tessa's voice was a wail. 'Because——'

'Leave it, Tessa, there's a good girl.' He was beginning to sound very tired now. 'I intend to have a good night's sleep and by daylight things will look quite different. I'm gong to crawl into the bathroom now, and then into bed and I think, in the circumstances, that we shall have to share it.' He began to ease his legs off the sofa.

'Oh, I could——' Tessa began.

'Kip down on the sofa? Why bother? Much too complicated to search for pillows and blankets and things in the dark. We're in this mess together, little Tessa, let's not put up barriers. I assure you I'm quite harmless and incapable tonight.' He yawned hugely.

'Oh, all right.' Tessa was much too tired, herself, to argue.

So ten minutes later she lay on the edge of the big bed, her outer clothes in a heap on the floor. On the other side of the bed Alaric was already asleep, breathing evenly. She turned towards the broad, naked back, wondering if she dare disturb him to pull the duvet further over herself. As it was she was only half covered and beginning to get very cold. She wriggled round, feeling the pull on her damaged shoulder as she moved.

Oh, she was so sleepy—so tired. Why be stupidly modest? Anyway, Alaric was too deeply asleep to be aware of her, or what she was doing. Cautiously she eased herself nearer to him until her body, in its flimsy pants and bra, was moulded against the warmth and firmness of his broad back. She lifted her hand and touched his shoulder. She heaved a deep sigh and her arm went round his body as she nestled against him. His skin was warm and smooth and slightly damp to her touch. How good it was to be close—how right. Her mind was swept clear of thought, she only knew that she was safe here, with this man, and that in some odd way the world was a more hopeful place than it had been for a long, long time.

Suddenly she felt overwhelmingly tired; tired and yet completely peaceful. It was as if they had just made love.

Her mouth was against the firm contour of his back. She could feel the shoulder-blade just below the skin;

here was no spare flesh on him anywhere. His
breathing was slow and even; he was fast asleep. And
with a little smile on her lips, Tessa slept too.

CHAPTER FOUR

IF TESSA dreamed she didn't know it. When she wakened her head was half buried beneath the duvet and as she blinked her eyes open she saw that it was full daylight. The memory of all that had happened last night unfolded, hazily at first and then with a shock of disbelief as she was aware of the warm bulk of a man's body, only inches away from her.

She lay very quiet, still only half awake. There was an almost painful longing to reach out and touch him. It would have been so right, so natural.

So—*crazy!* What are you thinking of, Tessa Durant? Haven't you had enough heartbreak, without letting yourself in for more of the same? For that was how it would be if she took Alaric Brent up on his offer of yesterday evening, just before the lights went out. You have to take people on trust, he had said. That was the way men looked at it.

She had trusted Marc. Trusted him with her body and everything else that made up her being. When it was over she had vowed that never again would she be so vulnerable, so childishly trusting. Never again would she let a man's magnetism reduce her to a quivering acquiescent *nothing*.

Alaric Brent had the same magnetism, the same physical attraction for her, she admitted it. Since Marc

74

no man had even vaguely got below her defences, although there had been several who had tried. She recognised the danger, and that was half the battle, wasn't it? There was no future for her with Alaric Brent, he wasn't a one-woman man. If she ever met a man she could trust it wouldn't be a man remotely like Alaric.

The thoughts went through her mind slowly, one by one, as she lay curled up under the duvet in the big bed, so close to temptation, steeling her will to resist it. For if she reached out and wakened him to her touch, caressed him even gently, she would be committing herself—promising——

When she heard the sound she thought she must be dreaming. A woman's voice was calling from somewhere across the room. 'Ricky!' And then, from nearer, 'Rick—wake up, lazy bones.'

Tessa froze. Beside her in the big bed she felt Alaric stir, grunt, and heave himself up. 'Cara—what the hell? What are you doing here?' Sleep slurred his words.

'I've come to have breakfast with you, darling. I've been driving since the crack of dawn. And—oh!' The words ended in a gasp.

Tessa's eyes appeared over the top of the duvet. Her black satiny hair was spread across the pillow. She had a wild desire to giggle. It was too absurd—like a French farce.

Cara. Cara Everett, the company secretary, the only visitor that Alaric was always willing to see, so Freda had said knowingly.

Tessa was in no state to take in details. She had an impression of a tall, fairish, well endowed young woman in black pants and a dazzling multicoloured, designer-style top. Her mouth was hanging open in an expression of stunned surprise.

For a moment she stood there gaping. In her gaudy jumper she reminded Tessa of a tropical fish staring through the glass wall of its tank. Then, without another word, she turned and rushed out of the room, slamming the door behind her.

Tessa wriggled out of bed and stood looking accusingly down at Alaric. 'You shouldn't have let her go like that. She's your girlfriend, isn't she?'

He eased himself on the pillows, wincing slightly as he did so, wide awake now. 'What should I have said? I believe the standard cliché is, "Don't go, I can explain everything." '

'It isn't funny. Shall I run after her—get her to come back?' Tessa's cheeks were pink with annoyance and embarrassment.

Alaric reached over and tweaked the strap of her bra, and his eyes travelled down to her lacy panties. 'Like that? I hardly think it would be advisable—or convincing.' He settled down more comfortably. 'No, Cara will have to draw her own conclusions. She came uninvited.'

'But of course you'll be able to explain. I mean, when she knows what happened she's bound to believe you,' Tessa urged.

His eyes twinkled with faint amusement. 'You're very anxious about my reputation, Miss Durant. Or is it my love-life that concerns you?'

'I don't care particularly about either,' she said impatiently. 'I just thought she'd be very hurt and it's such a silly misunderstanding.'

'Suppose we forget all about it.' Suddenly he didn't look amused any longer. 'We have more important things to think about. Cara Everett is a tough lady; she won't fret too much about that little episode. Now I suggest that you go and put some clothes on, because I find your appearance rather distracting.'

'Sorry,' Tessa said distantly. Any tender feeling she had felt for him after his accident had gone. He was a hard, insensitive man who treated his women with contempt. She was thankful that she wasn't one of them. 'Can you tell me where my overnight bag has been put?'

'It's still in the car, I'm afraid. You'll find a gown hanging behind the bathroom door, slip that on and go down and rescue your stuff. The car's unlocked.'

Tess found an olive-green towelling robe and got into it, pulling it tight round her waist and turning up the sleeves. Alaric burst out laughing when she came back into the bedroom. 'You look cuddly, like a green teddy bear.'

She stalked across the room, ignoring him, tripping over the hem just as she reached the door. His laughter followed her down the stairs. And to make things worse, an electrician's van pulled up just as she was opening the boot of the car. The three men getting out of it gave her very interested looks.

Pain shot through her shoulder as she tried to lug her bag out of the boot and she gave a sharp yelp. The tallest of the three men looked over and came across. 'Give you a hand, miss?' He had yellow hair and a nice smile.

'Oh, thank you, I've hurt my shoulder a bit. If you could carry my bag upstairs for me?' What did it matter if he wondered what she was doing in Alaric's flat? She was beyond caring.

He followed her upstairs and put down the case inside the living-room and Tessa thanked him. 'That's very kind of you—you've saved my life.' She gave him a lovely smile and he grinned widely. 'My pleasure, miss.'

It was annoying that she had to go through the bedroom to get to the bathroom. She opened her bag out on the floor and extracted jeans and a pale blue top and clean underwear. The bag itself could stay here, she certainly wasn't going to take it through into Alaric's bedroom. She had no intention of sharing the room with him again tonight.

'Who was that?' he said sharply as she went into the bedroom, carrying the garments over her arm.

She lifted her chin. 'One of the electricians, he was very kind and carried my case up when he saw that I was in difficulty.'

'Your shoulders! Oh, my poor darling, what a callous brute I am, I'd forgotten all about them.' He began to ease himself out of bed, as if he could somehow atone for his thoughtlessness.

Tessa gazed with horror at the great blue-black patches on both his legs. She dropped the clothes she was holding and was across the room in a moment. 'Get back into bed immediately. Don't you dare move until the doctor's seen you.'

He made a face at her. 'I've *been* out of bed, Florence dear, I crawled to the bathroom and back—it wasn't too difficult.'

'Oh, well——' she said reluctantly. 'Oh, well, don't do it again, until I can help you,' she finished weakly, her cheeks warm.

'Come here, Tessa,' he said in a deep quiet voice that drew her towards him irresistibly.

He reached under the sleeves of the gown and took both her hands in his. 'I don't think I thanked you properly last night for what you did. God knows what would have happened if you hadn't been here—I should probably have still been lying there. You're a lovely, kind, brave girl, Tessa. Thank you again.' He lifted her hands to his mouth and kissed them one by one, first on the backs and then on the palms. When he raised his head their eyes met and held and she felt that everything inside her was slowly melting. She had a reckless urge to sink on to her knees beside the bed and lift her mouth to his.

He shrugged slightly and released her hands. 'Now, run along and dress,' he said in an ordinary voice. 'Do you think you can manage, or are your shoulders too painful? I could probably help——'

'Oh, no.' Tessa picked up her heap of clothing and fled across the room. 'No, I can manage perfectly well. Thank you,' she added as an afterthought.

She heard Alaric chuckle as she closed the bathroom door. And she was almost certain that she heard him say, 'Some other time then. I'll look forward to it.'

What would Cara Everett make of that? Tessa wondered as she struggled to unfasten her bra.

And—more importantly—what did she make of it herself?

When Tessa came out of the bathroom, a quarter of an hour later, Alaric was speaking into the bedside phone. Her toilet had been fairly sketchy. Without any electric power the water in the taps was running cold and she was having enough trouble persuading her aching shoulders to function without risking a cold shower. A hot soak was what she needed. But she managed a quick sponge-down, and the mere fact of getting into fresh clothes had a stimulating effect on her spirits.

Alaric turned towards her when she opened the door into the bedroom and went on talking into the phone, at the same time raising his dark brows in obvious appreciation of her appearance.

'Really? That's very good of you. Yes, I'll expect you shortly. That's fine, and thanks very much, Bill. No, I promise to stay put until you arrive. Goodbye for now.'

He replaced the receiver. 'Our local doctor,' he said to Tessa. 'He's a good friend of mine, I've known him for years. He's promised to come along straight away.' He leaned back against the pillows surveying her with approval. 'You look delectable in that outfit, Tessa—like a bluebell in spring. And I like your hair loose. It makes you look more approachable.'

At his unexpected compliment she felt as flustered as a schoolgirl. 'My hair needs a good wash after wallowing in the mud last night, only the water's cold. And I wasn't aware that I was unapproachable.'

'Only sometimes.' He gave her such a wicked look that for an awful moment she wondered if he had been awake last night when she snuggled up to him in the big bed.

Her heart began to thump and she changed the subject quickly. 'Have you heard any news from Barney?'

Alaric nodded. 'I rang the hospital first and was able

to speak to him. He's been there with Mona all night. She'd had a good sleep and the baby's OK so far, and Mona's feeling very cheerful this morning. I told Barney more or less what had happened here and he's going to pick up a taxi to get to his cottage and then come straight on here. So after the doctor's been we can make some plans. Meanwhile, suppose you go down and contact your friend the electrician and see if he can do something about the generator.' His mouth twisted a little as he added, 'Give him that smile of yours and he'll be eating out of your hand.'

'Sexist stuff! I don't descend to that sort of thing.'

She pulled a face at him and ran down to the lab, where she found the yellow-haired electrician working on bundles of colour-coded wires in a box mounted on the wall.

'Please, could you help?' Tessa asked rather diffidently. 'I'm sorry to interrupt, but the generator seems to have gone wrong and we've had no power in the house since yesterday evening.'

The young man needed no persuading, and they went out together to the barn which housed the generator. As they walked Tessa explained briefly what had happened on the previous night.

'You mean, Mr Brent got himself mixed up with this little lot?' The young man surveyed the jumbled heap of logs lying outside the barn. 'Crikey, he'd have been killed if they'd come down on his head. What's the damage, then?'

Tessa told him that Alaric's legs were badly bruised and that the doctor was coming to examine him.

The electrician, who said that his name was Ted,

seemed genuinely upset. Was there anything he could do to help? Tessa said, No, she didn't think so at the moment, except that it would be useful if they could have some hot water. 'Well, then, miss, I'll get the generator fixed right away. And if it's something that's going to take a while, I'll down tools in the lab and get the mains going for you instead.'

'Oh, thank you, Ted, you're being a real help.'

Tessa smiled her nicest smile and Ted flushed bright red and muttered, 'My pleasure,' as he disappeared into the barn. All right, Alaric Brent, so it works, but I shan't give you the satisfaction of admitting it. In fact I shan't give you any satisfaction at all, and that's a warning. You can keep your winning ways for your girlfriend.

She wondered where Cara Everett was. There were only the Jaguar and the electrician's van in the drive, so she had evidently left in a huff. Tessa hoped she had driven straight back to London and wasn't still around, nursing her sense of outrage. It was up to Alaric to explain to her what had happened and she, Tessa, wanted to have nothing to do with it.

Before she went upstairs again she decided to explore the grounds. She needed a few breaths of sea air to steady her down.

The old house was a gem. At the back, its huge grey-stone bulk rose solid and impressive against the washed blue of the sky. Long bay windows of what was now the lab looked out across sloping lawns, sheltered on the left with a tall bank of pine trees. There were roses burgeoning red and white and cream in the centre bed, and at the bottom of the lawn a path between two clumps of feathery tamarisk led to a low stone wall at the very edge of the cliff. Tessa stood revelling in the view that presented itself. Far below the sea sparkled silver in the early morning sunshine. Small white-sailed boats were already skimming over the water. A strip of pale sand followed the curve of the bay, and on the horizon there was the misty shape of a land-mass which must be the Isle of Wight. She lifted her head and breathed in the sharpness and cleanness of the morning air. Already she loved this place; it would be crazy to turn down the chance of working here just because of a man whom she would hardly ever see. She couldn't wait to get started on her new job.

She walked back up the lawn and round the side of the house. Here she passed more rose-beds and a kitchen garden, greenhouses, and finally the garage buildings before she arrived back at the front door. Upstairs again, she found that Mrs Measures—presumably a kind of daily housekeeper—had arrived and was standing at the bottom of Alaric's bed, arms folded across a bright pink blouse covering an ample bosom, and volubly expressing both horror and sympathy at once at the tale which Alaric had evidently been unfolding.

She turned as Tessa walked in, and Alaric introduced them. 'Well, and you're the young lady as Mr Alaric's been telling me about, the one who saved him. What a dreadful thing to happen! It's quite turned me up to hear about it. A mercy you're both safe and sound. Now, Mr Alaric, you stay right where you are and rest your poor legs, and I'll make you a nice breakfast. There's bacon in the fridge, I shopped in when I knew you was coming.' She beamed at Tessa. 'Mr Alaric always likes his bacon for his breakfast and I dare say you could manage some yourself, me dear.'

'Mrs Measures grills a pretty rasher,' Alaric grinned. 'Thanks, Mrs M; the only thing is, the electricity's still off.'

Mrs Measure's hands went up in dismay. 'Oh dear, oh dear, and what about all the stuff in the freezer, and the milk and everything?' she wailed.

At that moment, right on cue, there was a kind of grunt from the direction of the kitchen, followed by a low humming, announcing that Ted had done his stuff and the various electric appliances were once again functioning. A relieved Mrs Measures departed to cook breakfast.

Tessa felt suddenly shy. She picked up Alaric's coat and trousers and hung them over the back of the chair, not looking at him. 'Well, and how are you feeling?' she enquired in a bright, nurse-like tone.

'Oh, fine, fine. I'll be leaping round like a mountain goat in no time at all.' But as she glanced at him she saw that he winced when he tried to shift his position in bed, and that his face was pale and drawn.

She said quickly, 'If I stick a couple of pillows under the duvet it would take the weight off your legs.'

'Oh, don't fuss, Tessa, I'm OK.' He was suddenly irritable.

She ignored that and took the pillows she had slept on last night and, lifting the bottom edge of the duvet, placed them one each side of his feet. 'How's that?'

'Better,' he admitted rather ungraciously. And then, 'Bear with me, Tessa. I'm not used to being an invalid, and I'm not enjoying it.'

Tessa had once nursed Marc through a bad attack of

influenza, which held him up in the middle of an important bit of research. No invalid could have been worse than he had been, snarling and griping at her until she had had to go out of the room to have a little weep in private. Alaric was at least trying to be civil.

'Would you like to shave?' she enquired.

He stuck out his chin with its twenty-four-hours' dark growth on it. 'Do I look like a yob?'

She put her head on one side. 'More like one of the smugglers you were telling me about. I can just see you climbing up the rocks on a moonless night with a crate of booze on your shoulder.'

'Charming. Well, lovie, I'm afraid you'll have to put up with it, because my razor plug is in the bathroom. And you've forbidden me to move out of my bed again,' he added smugly.

He grabbed her hand as she passed the bed and drew her towards him. His grip was steel-strong and she had no power to resist. 'Sexy smuggler, yes?' Pulling her head down he rubbed his scratchy chin against her smooth cheek.

'No,' said Tessa firmly. To him this was just fooling, and she felt she would die with humiliation if he guessed the effect the enforced intimacy was having on her. She would have to act the nurse for the moment. Kind but firm and having no nonsense with the male patients. 'Please let me go, Mr Brent, before Sister sees us.'

Mrs Measures came in with a tray of coffee at that moment and put it down on a small table by the window, tactfully ignoring the way that Tessa straightened up and moved away from the bed. 'I've made you both a nice big jug of coffee, and the bacon's nearly ready.'

'Can't I help?' Tessa asked.

The housekeeper gave her a doubtful look and then evidently decided that a girl who could save her dear Mr Alaric from disaster was to be trusted in the kitchen. 'Well, miss, if you could help me carry the trays in?' she suggested, and Tessa felt that she had made a friend.

Breakfast was only just over and the trays carried back into the kitchen when there was a loud knocking at the front door. A breezy voice called, 'Hello, anyone in?' and a stocky, middle-aged man carrying a black doctor's bag walked into the bedroom. Tessa thought he looked more like a farmer than a doctor; certainly he brought with him a whiff of the great outdoors.

He strode over to the bed and looked down at Alaric, his eyes accusing under bushy fair brows. 'Well, me lad, and what have you been getting up to? Haven't seen you laid up since you had measles when you were twelve and sent your poor grandmother spare with trying to get you to stay in bed.' He chuckled and looked questioningly across the room at Tessa, who was silently making for the door into the living-room.

'Stop a minute, Tessa,' Alaric ordered, and when she turned, 'Meet my good friend Doctor Hurley. Bill, this is my secretary, Tessa Durant, who pretty well saved my sanity, if not my life, last night, when I got myself pinned down under a stack of ruddy big logs. She managed to lug them off my legs, God knows how, and I'd like you to take a look at her and make sure she hasn't damaged herself.'

The doctor held out a large hand and Tessa put her own into it, wincing a little at the pressure. He turned her hand over and looked at scratches on the palm, frowned, and then said, 'H'm. We'll see about you later, young lady.'

Tessa smiled nervously and escaped into the living-room. What a muddle it all was, she thought, and how were they going to straighten it out? She walked across to the window and stood looking out across the garden to the strip of blue sea that was visible above the bank of tamarisk, waiting for the doctor to come in.

He appeared in a surprisingly short space of time and came across the room to her. In answer to her unspoken question he said briskly, 'He's not in too bad a shape, Miss Durant. We'll have to have him in for X-rays, just to make sure, but if there are no fractures showing up then it's just a matter of taking it easy for a few days until the bruising goes down. There's always a certain amount of swelling with a case like this, which might lead to complications, and he should rest as much as possible.'

'Yes, of course,' Tessa murmured. The doctor seemed to be taking it for granted that she was the one who was going to be in charge of Alaric. The prospect filled her with alarm. 'You—you don't think he needs a nurse?' she ventured.

Dr Hurley guffawed. 'Nurse? Lord, no, he'd have a fit at the suggestion. I gathered that he thinks a secretary will be much more to the point, and that's you, Miss Durant.' He slid her an enigmatic look—understanding rather than leery. 'And of course there's the estimable Mrs Measures to coddle him as well. No, he'll do very nicely. Now, let's take a look at you.'

Tessa submitted to a very thorough examination.

'You may not think this is necessary,' the doctor remarked, prodding her ribs and her stomach, 'but the lad in there would never forgive me if I missed anything. No, Miss Durant, I can't find any damage. Your shoulders and arms will be a bit stiff for a day or two, and your hands have suffered slightly, but you must have been in very good shape to cope the way you did.'

'I've been going to keep-fit classes,' Tessa told him. 'I expect that's kept my muscles in trim.'

The doctor packed his bag and snapped the lock as Tessa pulled her blue silky top over her head and down over her slim hips. He opened the door into the bedroom and called across the room. 'Can't find any damage to your young lady, you'll be glad to know, Alaric. I must be off now—we'll have a car along for you as soon as it can be arranged and get that X-ray done, and then you should be in the clear, but I'll be in touch and call back tomorrow. So long, both of you.' And with a cheery wave of his hand he had gone.

Tessa went back into the bedroom, looking accusingly at Alaric. 'Why did you tell the doctor that I'm your secretary?'

He smiled winningly at her. 'Because you will be, won't you, Tessa, just on a temporary basis, while I'm—so to speak—grounded. Please. There's work to do here. I haven't dared go into my office yet but I bet the desk's brimming over. Do be a kind girl and say you'll help out—I need you.'

That was what Marc had said: *I need you.* The way men manipulate women who love them. Emotional blackmail—the thing that she had vowed never to fall for again. She must make a stand and not allow herself to be manipulated. All the more so, because she didn't love the man, did she? Did she?

Then she met Alaric's smoke-grey eyes smiling wheedlingly at her under their long dark lashes and reluctantly she smiled back at him. She mustn't lose her sense of proportion—or her sense of humour. This was a little thing he was asking of her, not a thing that would shatter her reputation and ruin her chosen career.

'Will you, sweet Tess?' he pleaded.

She sighed and shrugged. 'I suppose I can bring myself to bash a typewriter for a little while longer.'

'Excellent!' he beamed. 'We're beginning to get things organised.'

You're getting *me* organised you mean, thought Tessa, asking herself again why she was putting up with it. But as she went to find the office, under Alaric's directions, she had a horrid suspicion that she knew.

Barney turned up half an hour later, looking more relaxed this morning. In reply to Alaric's immediate enquiry he said that the emergency seemed to be over and that the doctors were satisfied with Mona's condition for the moment. She would have to stay in bed, probably until the baby was born.

'She's chafing about that, rather.' He shook his head, worriedly. 'I'm afraid when she gets home she'll be getting up and doing too much.' He turned to Alaric. 'But what about you? What have you been doing to yourself?'

He sat astride a small bedroom chair, looking from Alaric to Tessa, as Alaric recounted the events of the previous evening. Tessa stood looking out of the window, a little embarrassed because she thought that

Alaric was putting far too much emphasis on her own part in them.

'What a girl!' Barney said admiringly as she turned and gave him a smile and a head-shake that discounted Alaric's fulsome praise. 'Anyway, I'm glad it was no worse. It might have——' He broke off, looking quite shattered. 'So—what's the drill now? What's the damage?'

'I've got to go in for an X-ray,' Alaric told him. 'They're going to send an ambulance car for me when they can arrange it.'

Barney thought for a moment. 'Why don't I drive you into the hospital? If you'll trust me to drive your Jag, that is. I came straight here in the taxi and my car's still at the cottage.'

Alaric, impatient to get the X-ray over and done with, agreed and, after a phone call cancelling the ambulance car, Tessa left Barney to help Alaric to dress and get downstairs, and went back to the office to begin to put the desk in some sort of order.

Presently she heard shuffling footsteps on the landing and went to the office door. Alaric was leaning hard on Barney, while the tall man had to stoop from his enormous height to take the weight.

'Good luck!' Tessa called across the landing and Alaric turned and grinned and raised two thumbs before he began to tackle the stairs.

The office window overlooked the front of the house and Tessa stood there clutching the curtains and watched as Alaric came cautiously down the outside stone steps and eased himself into the Jaguar. How he must hate this, she thought, and the scene below misted before her eyes as a sudden wave of tenderness swept over her. Heavens, she was beginning to feel maternal towards him, that would never do.

The men had been gone for an hour or so and Mrs Measures had just brought Tessa in a cup of coffee, when footsteps sounded on the wooden staircase outside the office door, which was half open.

Tessa glanced round to see Cara Everett standing at the top of the stairs. Seeing Tessa, she walked in and stood staring across the desk with the slightly protuberant cold blue eyes that made Tessa think again of a fish in a tank. Her light brown hair was cut very short, very stylishly, and the multicoloured top strained tightly over an eye-catchingly expansive bosom.

Men were supposed to like that sort of shape, weren't they, Tessa thought. She said coolly, 'Mr Brent's not here, Miss Everett.'

The carefully outlined brows rose. 'You know who I am, then?'

'Oh yes. You're Cara Everett, the company secretary, from Head Office.' Tessa looked back at the letter she was reading.

After a pause the other girl said, 'So you're an employee, someone that Alaric brought here with him.'

'Yes,' said Tessa.

'Ah, that explains something.' Cara Everett sat down in the visitor's chair and crossed her elegantly trousered legs. 'I think you and I had better have a little talk then, as you're going to be working here.'

Tessa had a very good idea what was coming next, but she remained silent.

The blue eyes narrowed slightly. 'Naturally, you

know why he brought you here.'

'To do a job, of course. I'm a chemist.'

'Really? That makes a change. To do a job—yes, but what sort of a job? Doubtless the kind of job that dear Alaric expects of a girl who takes his fancy. And it's not in a laboratory, of course, it's in his bed, where I found you earlier.'

Tessa put down the letter she had been pretending to read and got to her feet. She felt more at ease looking down on this—this fishy woman. 'Miss Everett,' she said coldly, 'I realise that you must have got the wrong idea when you burst into the bedroom this morning, but I'm sure that Mr Brent will explain everything when you see him. There was a very good reason why I was sharing his bed.'

The other woman smiled thinly. 'I'm sure there was, but I really don't need any explanation. I quite appreciate that it will suit him very well to have a girl available when he has to be here for business purposes. I merely don't want you to get any wrong ideas. You must understand that Alaric Brent is mine—we've been lovers for years and it suits both of us that way. We neither of us put marriage before our careers, you see, and the arrangement leaves us both free to——' she shrugged delicately '—look elsewhere now and again. Variety lends spice, don't you think, Miss—er——'

Tessa crossed to the filing-cabinet and pulled out a drawer. Without looking round she said, 'I'm really not interested, Miss Everett.'

She slid the files along their rails, seeking for an imaginary document and presently she heard the other woman get up and go out of the room. Tessa went over and closed the office door and returned to the desk. There was a painful tightness behind her ribs and she made herself take a few deep, even breaths.

She wasn't in the least surprised, she told herself, and she had no reason to doubt what that hateful woman had said. The aching feeling inside was merely her way of reacting to aggression. She had never been very good at that.

The Everett woman must have gone along the passage to Alaric's private apartment—probably she hadn't believed Tessa when she told her that he wasn't there. She was away only a few minutes and then the footsteps returned along the passage, halted for a moment outside the office door, and then went on down the stairs. Tessa refused to allow herself to look down from the window, but she heard the sound of a car engine being revved up showily, and the crunch of gravel, and she sat quite still, seething with anger, until the sound faded in the distance.

There was a knock on the door and Mrs Measures came in, obviously fuming with umbrage, her cheeks nearly as pink as her blouse. 'Who does she think she is?' she burst out indignantly. 'Walking into my kitchen without so much as a by your leave, trying to quiz me. I never did think much of that woman, miss. Mr Alaric would be well rid of her.'

'She's the company secretary, Mrs Measures,' Tessa said, trying her best to sound reasonable. 'I suppose she considers that she had a special position here.'

'Special position!' echoed the housekeeper tartly. 'She thinks that, all right, always has done when she's

been hanging round Mr Alaric here. Has she gone?'
She stumped over to the window and glared down.
'Good riddance to bad rubbish,' she said feelingly.
And then, composing her features as she turned back
to Tessa, 'Now, what do you think you and Mr Alaric
would fancy for your lunch, miss, when he gets back
from the hospital?'

Lunch time came and went and Alaric hadn't
returned. Mrs Measures brought Tessa a tray into the
office, with ham sandwiches and salad and a mug of
coffee. 'Must keep your strength up, miss, specially
after what you went through last night.' She nodded
her approval.

Mrs Measures would approve of anyone who saved
her dear Mr Alaric, Tessa thought; it's obvious that
she adores him.

When the housekeeper had gone she sat for a long
time staring out of the window, the sandwiches
forgotten, until the dark green of the pine trees
blurred into the blue of the sky as thick tears gathered
in her eyes.

And so do I, she admitted at last, and pressed her
hands against her stomach as she felt a pang there of
something that felt like fear. Heaven help me, so do I.

It was nearly four o'clock when Tessa heard the
sound of the car approaching up the short drive. She
had spent most of the hours since lunch imagining the
awful things that could be happening. Alaric had been
kept in hospital. The X-rays had disclosed something
terribly wrong that Dr Hurley had missed. Appalling
pictures rose before her eyes of Alaric a hopeless
invalid, Alaric condemned to spend the rest of his life

in a wheel-chair.

She plunged down the stairs and was out in the drive as the Jaguar drew up. Just the sight of him, alive and sitting in the car, was enough to send an almost painful thrill through her body.

She couldn't wait for him to get out of the car; she pulled open the door on the passenger side and asked breathlessly, 'Well, how did it go? What's the result?'

The grey eyes passed over her face, as if he were learning her features by heart. Then Alaric smiled his slow, heart-wrenching smile and reached out and put his hand against her flushed cheek.

'You really do care, don't you?' he said, so softly that Barney, on the other side of the car, couldn't hear his words.

'Of course I do,' Tessa whispered fiercely. 'Didn't I pull you out from under the pik-a-stiks?' She mustn't embarrass him by showing too much emotion. She remembered how Marc had hated that.

'So you did. Well, you'll be happy to know that your efforts were rewarded. No fractures, no crushed bones, only a variety of gorgeous bruises which are rapidly taking on the hues of a colourful sunset. As the good doctor suggested, I have to rest up for a day or two and then I'll be as good as new.'

Relief washed over her like a great wave. She wanted to shout and throw her arms around him. But Barney had joined them now and she had to be satisfied with a heartfelt, 'That's marvellous. I'm so glad.'

Alaric was still sitting back in the car with his eyes

fixed on her face, and she suddenly felt ridiculously shy. 'I—I suppose you've had lunch, have you?' was all she could think of to say.

'A pub lunch,' Barney told her. 'To celebrate. And by the way we called at your cottage on the way back to make sure that it's ready for you when you want to move in.'

'Oh,' said Tessa blankly. She had forgotten all about the cottage. She had forgotten everything except that Alaric was here and that she could look at him and touch him and hear his voice.

'I'll go and see about some tea,' she muttered and hurried upstairs.

Alaric climbed the stairs much more easily than he had descended them a few hours earlier. Very soon he was ensconced on the sofa in the living-room and Tessa was insisting that he put his feet up. She arranged cushions behind his back, and assumed her mock-severe nurse's voice to say, 'And there you'll stay, Mr Brent. Doctor Hurley left you in my charge and I'll see that you behave yourself.'

'Not much hope of doing anything else, maimed as I am.' Alaric threw a pathetic glance at Barney.

This was all light stuff, of course, but Tessa saw the rather puzzled look that Barney cast from one to the other of them. He was obviously wondering about the relationship between them.

Which wasn't surprising, Tessa thought. She was wondering herself. There was only one thing she was resolved that it wouldn't be. And there was no prize for guessing what that was.

She might be falling in love with Alaric Brent—indeed, she might have already fallen in love with him—but he certainly wasn't in love with her. So she must guard her heart, because there was no future for them together.

CHAPTER FIVE

'NOW, what's the drill?' Barney asked, finishing his last cup of tea. 'I must get back to the hospital by six, but until then I'm free. Why don't I take Tessa along and show her the cottage? Then, if she agrees, she could borrow my car to drive back here and I could hang on to your Jag for a day or two, Alaric, until you're fit to drive yourself.'

'Brilliant,' Alaric agreed. He looked at Tessa. 'Are you prepared to take up residence?'

'I'd like to see the cottage,' she said cautiously, her mind busy with the implications of this arrangement. If she moved into the cottage then Alaric would be left alone all night in this big empty house. She imagined him falling, perhaps trying to get to the office along the passage, and hurtling down the stairs, and her stomach went hollow.

To her relief Barney took up the point before she had to do it herself. 'There's got to be someone here tonight, boss,' he told Alaric. 'We can't have you taking the risk of being on your own in case of an emergency. You're not too steady on your pins yet. I could stay myself, only ——' He looked questioningly from one to the other of them.

Alaric's eyes met Tessa's. 'Tessa's nominated herself as my nurse,' he said. 'What more could I need?'

There was a mischievous glint in his eye and she knew what Barney must be thinking. She wanted to say, 'Look, Barney, Alaric's just having his little joke, for reasons best known to himself. He and I aren't sleeping together, however it may seem.' But that would be embarrassing for Barney, as well as for herself, so she had to pretend not to notice the challenge. If Alaric wanted to play silly games, she told herself crossly, let him get on with it. But she hadn't missed the look that passed between the two men. I could murder him for this, she thought furiously, glaring at him. In return he gave her a melting look—the picture of innocence.

Enough of this, she thought impatiently, and started to put the tea things together on the tray. She carried it into the kitchen, which was tidy and empty. Mrs Measures evidently left in the afternoons when she had prepared tea.

'Be with you in a few minutes,' she called back to Barney, and went through to the bathroom, where she had parked her travelling-case. Here she changed from jeans into the skirt of her navy linen suit, swilled her face and renewed her make-up.

Back in the living-room she took her jacket from the back of a chair, where she had hung it yesterday, and slung it around her shoulders. 'Ready when you are,' she told Barney. 'I mustn't be away too long myself, I'm looking forward to having a bath and washing my hair when I get back. The water should have hotted up by then.' She turned to Alaric. 'Can I get you anything before I go?' she enquired solicitously.

'Something to read?' She went across and ran her fingers along the books in the bookcase beside the window. 'Here you are — *War and Peace.* That should keep you amused for an hour or so.' She placed the outsized tome on his knees. 'Now don't you dare move until I come back,' she ordered sternly. 'Promise.'

He grinned up at her. 'Cross my heart,' he said, reaching for her hand and placing it against his chest. 'Feel it beating?'

She could feel his ribs though the thin shirt, his heart beating, strong and regular, and her own heart responded with a wild leap. She pulled her hand out of his grasp. 'I wish you wouldn't,' she said confusedly, glancing over her shoulder and grateful to see that Barney had gone ahead of her out of the room.

'I like to see you blush,' Alaric told her wickedly. 'And an invalid must have his little amusements.'

Then suddenly is face changed and he wasn't smiling any more. 'I warn you, Tessa, if I stop making a joke of this, I shall be intolerable, so if you don't want me to start bawling you out, I'd advise you to enter into the game,' he said curtly.

She stared at him, seeing the anger—violence almost—that he was keeping bottled up, and a spasm of fear gripped her stomach. This was the real man, the dark, dangerous man she had first recognised. The light teasing was just a game he played because he found himself involved in a situation with her that might become an embarrassment to him.

A game! Anything that happened between them would be in the nature of a game. She mustn't forget that, mustn't ever take him seriously, because if he looked at her with anger and contempt she would die.

She nodded, her mouth firming. 'OK, she said. 'I'll remember.' And she followed Barney down the stairs.

It was a little after six o'clock when Tessa got back. Alaric was still lying on the sofa where she had left him, and when she went into the room he blinked at her as if he had just woken up.

It had come on to rain while she was out and the sky was overcast now. She switched on the light and said brightly, 'Well, how's the invalid?' She had made up her mind during the time she had been out that she was going to keep her cool and not allow Alaric to provoke her.

But neither was she prepared to play games with him. Definitely no flirtation, because that spelled danger—to her, of course, not to him.

He smiled across the room at her from his position on the sofa. 'I think the proper term is "resting comfortably", isn't it?'

'Good,' she said briskly. 'That's what I like to hear. She sat down on a small chair near the sofa. 'Have you enjoyed *War and Peace?*' Oh dear, this sounded dismally like a hospital duty-visit, where the visitor sits and racks her brains, trying to think of something to say.

Alaric regarded her soberly. 'I haven't been reading,' he said. 'I've been thinking.'

'Oh, yes?' She fixed an interested expression on her face.

'Yes, Tessa, thinking. I've been thinking that there's been enough war between you and me, on and off, and it's time to declare peace. I've been thinking that I've got off on the wrong foot with you. Believe me, I didn't mean to. I respect you, Tessa. That may sound very old-fashioned but it's the truth. I've every reason to be grateful to you and you've every reason to object when I behave so crassly. Will you call a truce and let's start again and be friends?'

Friends! That was what she had wanted once—in another life—before she fell in love with him.

Her eyes searched his face, seeing the sincerity there, valuing it and longing to see something entirely different. How would he look at a woman he loved? She could almost imagine that the long, mobile mouth softened into tenderness, that there was a blaze of passion and longing in the smoke-grey eyes. She felt a shiver run through her and she stood up quickly. 'Of course we'll be friends,' she said. 'I've been stupidly touchy. I was angry because you gave Barney the wrong idea.'

'What wrong idea?'

'About—us,' she said awkwardly.

'Yes, I suppose I did. This whole business has thrown me rather, and I took refuge in flippancy. Or——' he gave her a wry grin '—it might have been a Freudian slip. You know, wishful thinking.'

'You're doing it again,' she accused him. She placed her feet together, folded her hands on her lap, and met his eyes coolly. 'Look, Alaric, you know I'm not in the market for casual affairs, I've made no secret about that. I'm not expecting you to make a pass at me and it won't hurt my vanity if you don't. So while we're here together you'll just have to think of me as a—as a male nurse.'

He gave a loud guffaw of laughter. 'My dear girl, have you looked at yourself in the mirror lately? However——' he composed his features '—I'll do my best to take this situation seriously and respect your wishes. I shan't need any nursing, male or otherwise. The medicos say I can make my own way round the flat, just so long as I rest most of the time until the swelling goes down. Doctor Bill is going to look in tomorrow and hopefully he'll sign me off in a few days. So until then I promise not to look at you more than I can help. If you could wear trousers it might make it easier for me—you have the most beautiful legs,' he added casually. He might have been referring to a Chippendale chair. 'We shall have plenty of work to occupy us. How did you find the office?'

'Littered, as you expected.' She felt a certain relief that he was being sensible about all this. If they could keep off personalities she might be able to endure these few days in his company without losing her head completely.

'Now, how about if you get us both a drink,' he said 'and then come and sit down and tell me the news. Did you drive the Escort back?'

She poured a large whisky for him and a thimbleful for herself and returned to her chair. 'Yes,' she said. 'No problem—it's the same model and year as Daddy's. I drove to the hospital in front of Barney, so that he could keep an eye on me. While I was there I saw Mona for a minute or two, and I think we'll hit it off splendidly.'

He nodded, pleased. 'And what did you think of the

cottage?'

There was no need to hide her delight about this. 'It's lovely,' she said, her eyes shining. 'I shall look forward to staying there. It's so tiny—like a doll's house—and the view from the front window is simply fabulous, with the hill rising up behind and the sheep grazing. Is it very old?'

'Pretty old. That row of cottages originally belonged to a farm, which has now disappeared. It's all National Trust land now, and my grandfather bought the cottages when they came up for tender. They were very run down and he made quite a hobby of restoring them. When I made my plans for the lab here I thought it would be a good idea to finish the modernisation and furnish them completely for some of the staff. Three of the cottages are larger—yours is the little one in the middle.'

'I'm lucky,' Tessa said, and he smiled into her eyes—not challenging, not flirting, just unaffectedly pleased, as he replied,

'You deserve the best.'

This little episode between them marked a new beginning, Tessa told herself. They were friends. Cara Everett would have to believe that, but the thought wasn't satisfying, it was utterly bleak. She could imagine that woman's thin, supercilious lips curling at the amusing idea of inspiring a man's respect. She heard again the contemptuous voice saying, 'Alaric Brent is mine—we've been lovers for years——' Oh, yes. Cara Everett and Alaric shared something quite different from friendship, and the thought of that was a dull ache in the region of Tessa's stomach.

She wondered if she should tell Alaric that Cara had come back when he was away in hospital, and decided against it. She doubted if she could speak that horrible woman's name without showing her disgust, and Alaric would certainly notice that and wonder . . .

She pushed away the painful picture that rose before her eyes, and got to her feet. 'I must phone my parents and explain what's happened. If my mother rings the flat and I'm not there she'll start to worry. Then I'm going to have a bath and wash my hair and after that I'll see what Mrs Measures has left for our supper. Is there anything I can get for you before I go?'

'If you'd just straighten my pillows, please.'

'Of course.' She put a hand behind his back to push him forward while she plumped up the pillows. Her cheek touched his thick brown hair as she bent over him and her knees went weak. Oh, God, she thought, this nursing business was going to be agony.

'That better?' she said brightly.

'Excellent, thanks.' He opened the volume of *War and Peace* and nodded at her with a grateful but dismissive smile.

And that, thought Tessa as she went into the living-room and picked up the telephone, set the tone of their relationship for the next few days. Impersonal—friendly. Well, that was what she wanted, wasn't it? She just hoped she could keep it up without giving herself away hopelessly.

As things turned out, the week that followed was both

easier and more difficult than she had expected. Alaric kept his promise, and he seemed to have no particular difficulty in treating Tessa as he would treat any business colleague. No more meaningful looks, no more sexy double-edged remarks. Not once did he take her hand or touch her. It was both a relief and a painful longing that got no better. She slept badly, not because the sofa wasn't beautifully comfortable—it was. Covered with a fluffy, light blanket, she tossed and turned, unable to forget that it was on this sofa that Alaric spent his days. She could imagine the imprint of his body, smell the clean, masculine smell of his skin and his hair. She longed for him with every bit of her, and it was torture to know he was lying in the big bed with only a thin wall between them.

The days were better. She put a low table beside the sofa and on this Alaric spread out his papers. He dictated answers to letters and began to put together a long and detailed report on the setting up of the laboratory and the work that would be done in it. He dictated to Tessa and she spent hours in the office at the electronic typewriter. He talked to her about his plans for the laboratory and she listened, fascinated, happy and flattered that he should take her into his confidence.

Barney divided his time between the laboratory and the hospital and came to the flat each evening for a meal and to report to Alaric on the progress of the work down in the lab. Mrs Measures prepared supper for the three of them before she left, and Tessa heated the food up and served it. Afterwards they talked, or watched TV or played records, and it was all easy and friendly. Later, Barney stood by while Alaric got himself into bed, and then he left for his cottage, while Tessa made up her own bed on the sofa in the living-room.

It was a good working arrangement, she congratulated herself, and she was fairly confident, now, that Barney hadn't got any wrong ideas about herself and Alaric.

Each day Alaric insisted on her going out for exercise and fresh air, and she began to know and love the part of Purbeck where the old house stood. She climbed up the steep grassy track above the house, which led to a cliff-top high above the sea, or made her way down to the beach and walked along the sand while the waves curled in at her feet. In June the older children were at school, but families with tiny children came to the beach and the children laughed and chased about with red and blue and yellow balls nearly as big as themselves and their parents sunbathed and swam and picnicked. Summer had come in earnest now, and the sunny days followed each other, and Tessa began to love the old house and its surroundings almost as much as Alaric did.

Soon she would have to return to London and make arrangements about her flat. Everything was rather vague at the moment, and she couldn't decide whether she should give up the flat or not. But at all events she must move some more clothes here. To tide her over, she drove Barney's Escort into the nearest town and bought another two sets of underwear, and a pair of linen trousers with a couple of modest tops. The very last thing she wanted to do was to wear anything that Alaric could construe as seductive.

She visited Mona at the hospital on several afternoons when Barney was at the laboratory and they talked babies together, and if Tessa felt sharp stabs of regret she was able to hide it. Her first impression of Mona was confirmed. She was a cheerful, no-nonsense girl with wonderful brown eyes and a delicious sense of humour, and she adored her tall, clever husband. Tessa looked forward to the time when Mona would be released from hospital and would come home to the cottage, and she herself would move in next door. Alaric planned to return to London as soon as the doctor allowed him to travel. When he had finally left and she didn't have to see him all day and every day, things would be different—and easier, she hoped.

She phoned her mother, in Devon. She felt guilty that she hadn't disclosed the full story—merely talking rather vaguely about a new job, and the cottage that was going with it, leaving out all the details of Alaric's accident. Her mother would be worried sick if she had any idea that Tessa was staying in a flat alone with a man. She would immediately jump to the conclusion that history was going to repeat itself.

'I'm fine,' Tessa reassured her, in reply to her mother's queries. 'This is a lovely spot, and I'm having a holiday by the sea in my spare moments. Now, don't *worry*. I'll write and tell you all about the job and my lovely little cottage and you and Dad must come and see it later on when I'm properly settled in. It's lovely that I won't be nearly so far away from you.'

At the end of the week Dr Hurley called and examined Alaric, and pronounced him fit to travel, but not to drive the car.

'Good,' Alaric said to Tessa when the doctor had left, 'so we'll go back by train tomorrow. Then you can pack up your things at your flat and we'll transport them up here next time we come—which will be fairly soon. Does that sound like a good arrangement?'

Tessa didn't reply at once. Then she said, 'I just wondered—if I stayed on here I could help with looking after Mona when she's discharged from hospital in a day or two. Barney was worried about keeping her in bed, and she really should obey doctor's orders. All her relatives and friends are in Australia and she hasn't got anyone in this country to help out. If I moved into the cottage next door I should be able to be with her most of the time, do the cooking and shopping for them and so on, which would release Barney to go on with his work getting the lab set up. What do you think?'

He nodded slowly as if she had confirmed something he had been thinking about himself. 'I think,' he said, 'that you're a very nice girl, Tessa Durant, and that it's a very good idea.'

He smiled at her, and there was something in his eyes that she hadn't seen there before. Not teasing, or irony, certainly not love. Admiration, perhaps, and friendship.

For some unexplained reason Tessa felt her cheeks going hot and she turned away quickly. 'I'll get back to the office,' she said. 'I must finish your letters for signing before you go.'

'So,' Alaric said, 'it's over, our little seaside idyll.'

It was late that same evening. They had had dinner and talked over plans. Barney had left, happy and grateful to Tessa for her offer, and Alaric had retired to his bed.

'Idyll!' Tessa poured out tea and handed him a cup. It had become a regular habit for Tessa to make tea last thing in the evening when they discovered that they both had a liking for it. 'It hasn't been much of an idyll for you.'

'Oh, I don't know, in a way I've enjoyed it.' He stretched out his long legs under the duvet and leaned back luxuriously. 'It's not been all bad. It's given me a chance to catch up with my paperwork—with the help of a very competent secretary, I may add. And also, it's given me a chance to get to know that same competent secretary rather better than I should have done in the usual run of things. Still,' he mused, 'it hasn't been the way I would have chosen to spend our time together here. There's so much I want to show you.'

Our time together here! He was talking as if they had planned a holiday together. Perhaps that was what he *had* intended at first—to get her here alone. To soften her up so that he would have a girl available when he had to be here on business. Just as Cara Everett had said. Tomorrow he would go back to London—to Cara. Jealousy cut through Tessa like a steel blade, and she gripped the arms of the basket chair she was sitting in as if they were dangerous snakes.

'We'll have it all to come later though.' Alaric sipped his tea and in the light from the bedside lamp his grey eyes were dreamy. 'The holiday months will be busy, but when the season's over and the tourists have all gone we'll have Purbeck almost to ourselves. October can be marvellous in these parts. We'll walk along by the sea—all the way to Shell Bay—and I'll collect those little silvery shells and make a necklace for you. And we'll climb over the heath and look for the eiderduck and the black-tailed godwits from Brand's Point—where the smugglers loaded their flat-bottomed boats. And I'll drive you up to the top of Creech Hill and we'll look down on the whole of Purbeck spread out below. Oh, there are lots of lovely places. I can't wait to show it all to you, Tessa.'

He smiled into her eyes and Tessa felt a delicious weakness run through her. This was just idle talk, she knew that, but for a moment she could let herself believe that it would all happen like that, the two of them together in the places he loved, wandering along the sands, their arms round each other like lovers; lingering in the loneliness of the heath to kiss, and perhaps to lie down in the heather——

She pulled herself together with an effort. 'It sounds fascinating. But I shall be working, not holidaying, had you forgotten?'

'Life's not all work,' he grinned, 'and you deserve some reward for your ministrations. You've suffered too—having to sleep on that sofa, when there's a perfectly good bed here that we might have shared. No!' He held up his hand when she would have spoken. 'Don't say it. I know the score. And you must admit that I've behaved beautifully. Kept all the rules that you made.'

'Oh, yes,' Tessa admitted with a light laugh. 'Your behaviour has been quite exemplary. Ten out of ten for good conduct.' She got up from her chair by the window and walked over to take his cup. 'Finished your tea? You should be settling down now, you've got a train journey tomorrow.'

She put out her hand for his empty cup, but before she could take it he had put it down with a clatter on the bedside table, and stretched out and caught her hand in his. His smoke-grey eyes met hers and held them and she couldn't look away. Suddenly there was a silence in the room—a silence that seemed to spread all over the big, echoing house. Tessa's heart gave a great throb, then began to thump against her ribs.

'It's been hellish difficult, behaving beautifully,' Alaric said huskily. 'Don't you think I merit a prize for trying? Just one small kiss, perhaps?'

She stared at him wide-eyed for a long, long moment. Then all the longing that she had suppressed in these last days welled up and engulfed her like a warm wave. He must have seen her weakness, for he held on to her hand and drew her down beside him on top of the duvet, and when she felt his mouth on hers there was no resistance left in her, she was all soft and melting. Oh, but she loved him. Nothing else mattered but this man and this moment.

Her arms went round his neck and he kissed her, very gently at first, almost wonderingly, as if he were unsure of her response, but when she kissed him back it was as if a coiled spring were released in him. He pulled her closer, his mouth closing hungrily over hers, savouring the sweetness there, moving from her mouth to her cheeks, her temples, closing her eyes with kisses, then burying itself in the warm hollow of her neck.

They were both trembling as Tessa clung to him with a mounting passion that had been growing unreleased and now broke from its bonds. She moaned faintly as his fingers fumbled with the buttons of her blouse, unclipped her bra so that it fell away and left her breasts free for his caresses.

Oh, God, she wanted this man. She wanted to be held against him—against the naked hardness of him—not like this, with the thickness of the duvet separating them. She was lost in a world where nothing mattered now but the need for union, for ultimate satisfaction. She slid sideways, pulled up the duvet and wriggled herself beneath it. They were together now, clinging together, their bodies quivering with unashamed desire. Her hands went round his neck, her fingers digging into his thick hair convulsively. She closed her eyes, moving and swaying with the waves of longing that washed over her. Then his mouth took hers again, almost savagely now, as the weight of his body covered hers, his hands on the zip of her jeans, then pulling them down round her ankles. 'I want you,' he groaned. 'It's been hell, wanting you so much.'

It's been hell wanting you so much. From a time long ago the words echoed in her mind, and she stiffened as they touched a chord of memory, like touching a raw, exposed nerve, sounding from far, far away, but so clear that it sent a shudder all through her.

Her head was tipped back on the pillow. She opened her eyes and in the shadowy light from the bedside lamp stared with a kind of horror into the man's face above her own. His features were tense with unashamed lust. His hair stood up in spikes above his ears where her fingers had raked through it, his eyes were half closed. They seemed to her feverish imagination to be leering at her erotically.

Panic claimed her, wild unreasoning panic. It was a devil looking down at her greedily—a terrifying devil.

A devil with Marc's eyes——

'No—no—' she screamed, terror galvanising her with enough strength to push him off her. She wrenched herself away and slid from the bed to the floor, where she lay, sobbing hysterically.

Dazedly she heard Alaric's smothered profanity, felt a stinging slap across her cheek, heard his furious voice shouting, 'Shut up, Tessa. For God's sake, shut up.'

She lay on the carpet, shaking, her teeth chattering, sick with shock and humiliation. Above her she could hear Alaric's quick, harsh breathing and knew that he had turned away, and was lying on his side with his back to her.

She dragged herself up until she was kneeling beside the bed. 'Alaric?' She forced the words out. 'I'm sorry, I didn't mean——'

He rolled over until their faces were on a level. The light from the bedside lamp shone on his face, ashen-white and drawn into such an expression of angry contempt that she hardly recognised him.

'Get out—clear out of my sight,' he snarled.

'You don't understand—let me explain——'

He pulled himself up in the bed until he was glaring down at her as she knelt below him. 'Explain! What the bloody hell is there to explain? For once you behaved like a real woman and then you changed your mind.'

'Why won't you listen to me?' she shouted at him, struggling to her feet. 'I wanted you. I love you. You've got to believe me.'

'Have I?' he sneered. 'Well, I don't want you any more, not after your recent performance. And I certainly don't love you. Now cover yourself up, for God's sake, and get out of my sight.'

'Oh!' Her teeth bit into her lower lip, still tingling from his kisses. 'You're unjust—cruel.'

'Probably,' he said, his mouth a thin, hard line. 'There's a word for you, too, my girl, only I'll spare you that. Now get out before I put you out.'

The heat had gone from her body now, leaving her icy cold. Numbly she reached down and dragged her jeans up and stumbled out of the room, holding them round her waist. As she closed the door behind her the bedside lamp went out. It seemed like a final dismissal.

Back in the living-room she pulled a blanket round her and lay curled up on the sofa like a sick animal, staring ahead, where the moonlight threw stark shadows into the corners of the long room.

Humiliation poured over her, wave upon wave. That she should have lost control of herself when she had worked all these months since Marc's death to change, to cultivate poise, confidence, to keep her emotions under wraps! She hated herself. Almost she could believe that she hated Alaric, but that wouldn't have been true. It was her own fault, all of it. He had merely asked for a kiss and she had made it plain she wanted more, and then changed her mind. God! how he must despise her.

For hours she lay tense, her body cold, her head beating with the thoughts that scurried though it like black ants, and became more chaotic as the night wore on. If only she could sleep! If only she could stop thinking about Alaric and how she had ruined the relationship that had been growing between them! They had been friends, they had shared something good, something that might just possibly have grown into a deeper bond. He had needed her—perhaps he might, in time, have come to love her. But she had thrown it all away.

With the utter hopelessness of that certainty the tears came again. She must have sobbed for hours, stuffing her mouth into the pillow so that no sound could be heard in the next room. Not that Alaric would be lying awake; he wouldn't waste any regrets on a girl who had behaved as she had done. It must seem to him the ultimate indignity, the ultimate insult. If only he knew the truth, she thought in despair. But she could never tell him now, and certainly he would never ask.

Some time before daybreak she fell into a heavy sleep and wakened to see the early morning sun shining redly through the uncurtained window. Alaric was leaving for London this morning, she reminded herself, trying to rub away the dull ache that encompassed the whole of her head. She was driving him to the station, it was all arranged. She mustn't let him down, or let herself down—any more than she had done already. Somehow she must play a part, act as she had never acted in her life before. It shouldn't be impossible, because she had no feeling now, no feeling in her body at all. There was ice running through her veins, not red blood. Perhaps if she thought of Cara Everett and her cool, sophisticated air, it would help. Cara Everett would never weep all night for any man, not even Alaric Brent.

Stiffening her resolve she pushed back the blanket and padded across the room to the bathroom. After her shower she dressed carefully in the jeans and white top that she had brought with her. She patted light powder make-up round her eyes, leaning to the mirror to search for tell-tale traces of the night that had passed. She paid fastidious attention to her hair, combing it back off her face severely, instead of leaving it loose as she had been doing recently. She must look immaculate this morning, cool and self-possessed.

When she was satisfied with her appearance she made morning tea and tapped on the bedroom door, ignoring the heavy beating of her heart. Alaric was out of bed, sitting on a chair beside the window, wearing his dark red dressing-gown. 'Good morning, Tessa. Ah, tea—good.' He accepted the cup she offered him. 'What should we do without our morning cuppa?'

So—it was going to be polite small talk this

morning, was it? The events of last night were to be
wiped out as if they hadn't happened.

Tessa drank her tea standing up. 'I've finished in
the bathroom and the water's hot,' she told him
brightly. 'I'll get breakfast while you're dressing. I
suppose we should start for the station about half past
eight.'

Mrs Measures wouldn't be here until nine and
Tessa set breakfast in the kitchen. She made toast and
coffee and grilled bacon for Alaric. He ate heartily and
didn't seem to notice that she was eating nothing at
all. He exuded good spirits this morning. 'It's great to
feel part of the human race again.' He flexed both legs
as he sat on the high stool at the breakfast bar.

'You'll be glad to see London again?' Tessa said
politely. Would he come back here soon? She didn't
know if she was going to be able to bear it if he
intended to visit the lab often, if she never knew when
she was going to see him.

'London? Oh, no, not particularly. I just want to get
into harness again.' He grinned at her amiably, just as
if nothing had happened to spoil the friendship they
had been building up over the last few days. 'I'll be
back here quite soon, you won't get rid of me as easily
as all that. I plan to have a little get-together when the
rest of the staff arrive and before the lab formally goes
into gear. I'll be in touch and perhaps you and Mrs
Measures would put your heads together and lay
on a few snacks, or nibbles, or whatever they're called.
I'll send in an order for the drinks cupboard to be
topped up.' He put down his napkin and consulted his
watch.

'I'll go and finish packing and join you down in the car in five minutes, OK?'

Tessa walked slowly downstairs. It was all so—so *domestic.* She might be any wife driving her husband to the station, giving orders to the domestic help, planning little parties. Only it wasn't like that and it never would be. She straightened her back, took a deep breath and went to get the car out of the garage.

Later in the day the roads would be busy with holidaymakers making for the coast, but early in the morning they were comparatively clear. Tessa drove carefully and in silence and Alaric didn't attempt to make conversation. When they arrived at the small station at Wareham Tessa pulled into a parking-bay and he said, 'Don't bother to get out, I'm not an invalid any longer, I can see myself off.'

He leaned over to get his bag from the back seat and Tessa drew away so that his arm wouldn't touch hers. He was going; this strange, painful episode was over. When they met again it would be as employer and employee; she would just be another member of staff.

He got out of the car and stood holding the door open, his head bent as he looked steadily at her. 'Tessa,' he said slowly, 'about last night.'

She held her breath, her eyes fixed on the lean, inscrutable face.

Then he shrugged. 'Forget it,' he said, and slammed the door.

She watched him walk across the roadway to the station entrance. He was limping slightly, and that sent a pang of tenderness through her, and her eyes misted. Before he disappeared into the booking-hall he turned and lifted a hand unsmilingly, and she raised her own hand like an automaton.

Then he was gone and Tessa reversed the car with a swish and drove back along the smooth white road through the heath as if all the furies in hell were after her.

CHAPTER SIX

FORGET it, he had said. Yes, that was the obvious thing to do, the sane, reasonable thing. But reason had nothing to do with being in love, and Tessa was deeply, almost painfully in love. Far from forgetting Alaric Brent, she thought of him all the time.

When she took possession of the cottage and celebrated her moving-in alone by the usual ritual of tea-making in the tiny, neat kitchen, he was there, lounging against the door-post, watching her, dark lashes lowering over smoke-grey eyes. When she drank her tea, sitting on the chintz-covered sofa in the living-room, he was sitting beside her, watching the sheep move slowly about the grassy hill that rose up steeply at the bottom of the front garden. When she climbed the narrow staircase that spiralled up to the one bedroom he was behind her. And when, weary but sleepless, she lay in the soft bed with the breeze from the open window cool on her cheeks, he was there too, holding her in his arms, telling her that he loved her.

It was all pure fantasy, of course, and she tried to laugh about it, but the laughter soon turned to tears. It seemed to her a bitter irony that she should shed more tears over Alaric Brent than she had ever shed over Marc.

Mona was discharged from hospital three days after Alaric left, and came home to the cottage next door. She had only been allowed to come home on the strict understanding that she would stay in bed and—as she had promised—Tessa took over the running of the cottage for her. She was glad to be busy and she began to regain some kind of balance as she filled her days with activity. She cooked and dusted and drove Barney's Escort into the town to shop, and generally made herself useful and kept a watchful eye on Mona.

'Chemist—secretary—nurse—housekeeper! My experience of life is certainly expanding,' she grinned cheerfully one day, a week after Alaric had left, as she carried morning coffee up to Mona.

Mona was sitting up in bed, her fair hair about her cheeks and her eyes shining with the special glow that impending motherhood bestows. 'I think you're marvellous. Absolutely——'

'Fair dunkum?' Tessa teased.

Mona pulled a face at her. 'We don't talk like that in Australia. Only in bad movies. No, Tessa, I'm serious. I think it's grand of you to stay on and keep me in order. There's something I want to ask you—will you be godmother to the infant?'

Barney came in from the lab just as Tessa was agreeing, and kissed his wife and took the mug of coffee that Tessa produced. 'Had to go into Wareham, so I called in to deliver the message for you, Tessa.'

Her heart leapt. Message? From Alaric?

'Your mother rang,' he said.

'Oh.' She let out her breath.

'She had only the number of the lab and I know

your phone's not connected here yet. She said she and your father would like to drive over to see you tomorrow and wondered if that would be convenient and if so could you ring her back?'

'Oh,' said Tessa again. 'Yes, of course. Thank you, Barney.' She passed her tongue over her dry lips; how idiotic to let herself hope.

'Barney,' she said after a moment's thought, 'would you—when you see my mother—would you mind not mentioning about Alaric's accident and about my staying at the flat to look after him?'

Barney was sitting on the bed, holding his coffee-mug in one hand, with his other arm round his wife. 'Ah,' he said knowingly. 'She'd think the worst, would she?'

'I'm afraid so.' Tessa pulled a wry face.

'Or the best?' Mona put in softly.

Tessa shook her head. 'No. No chance of that.'

'Are you sure, Tessa?' Barney looked hard at her.

'Quite, quite sure,' she said and took a gulp of hot coffee.

'Pity,' he said.

When he had left again Mona said, 'Alaric Brent's such a stunner. Barney thought that you and he—or am I speaking out of turn?'

'No, of course not.' Tessa shook her head wearily. 'Alaric was playing a silly game, letting Barney think that. Actually there's nothing between Alaric and me, nothing at all, except that I looked after him for a few days when he was hurt.' She picked up the coffee-mugs. 'I'll go down and see about lunch.'

The sun was shining when Tessa's parents arrived

next day. Her mother was charmed by the cottage. 'How lucky for you, darling,' she enthused, as Tessa was cutting bread and butter for lunch, having given Mona her lunch earlier and settled her down for her afternoon rest, 'and having a new job that you'll enjoy too.'

Her husband had gone outside to inspect the weedy garden, and Mary Durant lowered her voice. 'And what about Mr Brent, is he here?' She glanced over her shoulder as if she expected him to walk in at any moment.

'Oh, no,' Tessa said casually. 'He went back to London. He won't be working here, this laboratory is quite separate from the company's main premises. We're going to be engaged on a new project.'

Mrs Durant nodded and Tessa thought she looked rather disappointed. Alaric wasn't mentioned again and the rest of the afternoon passed off well. Tessa took her mother in to see Mona for a few minutes and then she drove both her parents to the lab, where she introduced them to Barney, and showed them the view from the top of the cliff.

As she said goodbye when they started on the return journey she decided that she must have put on a convincing show of pleasure and satisfaction. Her mother looked happier than for months past as she kissed her.

'I'm so very glad for you, my dearest. You deserve all the good luck you can get,' she said, and her father, who always left most of the talking to his wife, kissed Tessa affectionately and agreed.

She stood at the cottage door smiling as they drove

down the short grassy lane. At the junction her mother turned and waved out of the window and Tessa waved back enthusiastically. Then the car turned the corner and disappeared and the smile left Tessa's face abruptly. She shivered in the afternoon sunshine and went slowly back into the cottage.

Yes, she had convinced them. She had put on a good act and it would be practice for when she next saw Alaric, she thought desolately.

Mona's baby was born a week later, premature but healthy.

'She's heaven,' Tessa told Barney, when she went with him on the following afternoon to gaze at the tiny, perfect form in its protective bubble. 'Her little fingers and toes—they make me want to cry,' she sniffed.

Barney put an arm round her shoulders. 'Come and see Mona,' he said gruffly. 'She wants to thank you.'

'Thank *me?*' Tessa looked up, surprised, as they walked together along the corridor. 'Why ever?'

The tall man grinned down at her. 'She knows darned well that if you hadn't helped out as you have done, Tessa might not be here now.'

'*Tessa!*' she squeaked, stopping in her tracks. 'You're calling her after me?'

'Do you mind?' Barney urged her forward. 'It seems fitting.'

Tessa groped for her hanky. 'Now I know I'm going to cry,' she said.

Mona looked tired but blissful. When Tessa bent to kiss her she clung for a moment and their tears mingled. 'Hey, you two,' Barney remonstrated, 'you're breaking my heart.' And then they all laughed together and after that Mona had to open the parcel that Tessa had brought and hold the softness of the tiny white coat against her cheek, and hug Tessa again. The nurse came then to shoo the visitors out and Tessa waited in the car park for Barney to take leave of his wife.

He drove in silence, but it was a relaxed silence, and Tessa thought her own thoughts as the Jaguar purred softly along in the afternoon sunshine.

'I'm going to miss this little beaut.' Barney spoke at last, patting the steering-wheel lovingly as the car drew up outside Tessa's cottage—he himself intended to drive on to the lab. 'We'll have to see the garage about getting a little runabout for you when I take the Escort back from you tomorrow.'

'Tomorrow?' Tessa felt a painful throb deep inside her. 'Is Alaric coming for his car tomorrow?'

Barney switched off the engine. 'Yes, he's coming for this party affair, didn't you know? I though he'd have rung you.' Tessa's phone at the cottage had been connected for the last few days.

'There's no reason for him to ring me specially,' Tessa said rather shortly. Barney was evidently still taking it for granted that there was something going on between herself and Alaric.

'Sorry,' said Barney, 'I thought you knew about the party.' He looked crestfallen, and Tessa felt mean that she had snapped at him. It wasn't his fault that he had the wrong idea.

'No, *I'm* sorry, Barney,' she said quickly. She

hesitated and then went on, 'I know Alaric gave you the impression that he and I had—had something going between us, but it wasn't true, you know. He was just fooling.'

Barney nodded. 'I thought——' Then he shrugged. 'Oh, well, if you say so, Tessa.'

'I do,' she said, and smiled up at his nice, slightly embarrassed face as he sat with his hands on the wheel of the Jaguar. 'So the inauguration party for the lab is tomorrow, is it?'

'Yes, tomorrow evening. Mrs Measures is all of a flutter, although the eats and everything are being taken care of by a catering firm from Bournemouth.'

So Alaric had forgotten that he had suggested that she and Mrs Measures should arrange the party fare together. That hurt. It meant that he had shut her out of his mind completely.

'Alaric said he was getting a lift down tomorrow afternoon,' Barney told her. 'And we're all going to foregather at the lab at about six and drink to the new venture. And after that it'll be full steam ahead. I can't wait to get going. You're keen too, aren't you, Tessa? We'll have a good team.' There were to be eight of them in the team to begin with, counting a lab assistant and a young computer wizard.

'Oh, yes,' she said truthfully. 'I'm dead keen. I only hope I'll be able to live up to your standards.'

Barney nodded encouragingly at her as she got out of the car. 'You will, that's for sure,' he said. 'I recognise quality when I see it.'

'Thank you, kind sir,' she laughed. 'I'll be cooking something for supper later on. If you care to look in when you come back from seeing Mona there might be a bite going.'

'Thanks,' Barney told her. 'I may take you up on that.' He drove away with a cheery salute, and the laugh died abruptly on Tessa's lips.

A furniture van rolled up, and Barney had to pull the Jaguar into the bank to let it pass. The new occupants of the end cottage moving in, evidently. The cottage next door to Tessa's, on the other side from Barney's, was already occupied by a married couple, John and Sheila Clark. Tessa had had a few brief words with them yesterday and gathered that both husband and wife were medical biologists. They seemed pleasant, friendly people.

She hurried inside and shut the front door. It would be neighbourly to go and seek out the newcomers and offer any assistance they might need, but not now. She couldn't trust herself, at this moment, to be bright and sociable. Tomorrow she must go to the lab and see Mrs Measures and ask if she could help with the preparations for the party, but at this moment she had to be alone.

She prowled round the cottage restlessly. A good team, Barney had said, but would she be a member of it? It wasn't too late to change her mind, to do what she had orginally intended to do—walk out of any scene that contained Alaric Brent. She sank into a chair as her knees trembled. 'I can't. I can't,' she wailed aloud. The man was part of her, she could never walk out of any place where she might see him, if only for a moment, if only in the distance. It was weak. It was pathetic. She despised herself for it.

Tomorrow! It was too soon, it didn't give her time to prepare herself. She would have to see Alaric, probably have to speak to him. But there would be other people there, that might make it easier. Somebody was giving him a lift down from London in the afternoon, Barney had said. *Somebody*—Cara Everett, perhaps? She bit her lip so hard that she tasted blood.

This was ridiculous; she must get a grip on herself, find something to do. If she prepared a casserole now it would be cooked by the time Barney arrived. They would eat together and he would tell her about the baby, and they would talk shop about the lab, and the time would pass until she had to be alone.

This was going to be the pattern of her life for a long time to come. Filling every moment of the day so that she needn't think about Alaric. Weeping for him through the lonely nights. It was an all-too-familiar pattern.

Perhaps, she thought as she put out vegetables on the chopping-board, perhaps in some twisted, painful fashion, history *was* repeating itself. 'It's not fair!' She stamped her foot in a rare moment of angry self-pity. 'It shouldn't happen twice.'

A couple of hours later a savoury smell from the casserole was beginning to waft from the oven when there was a loud knock on the door. Barney was early this evening; or it might be one of the new neighbours. Pulling off her apron quickly Tessa hurried through the living-room and opened the door.

'Hello, I'm sorry, I'm——' she began.

Alaric stood outside the door. The taxi that had

evidently brought him from the station was reversing down the grassy track outside the cottages.

She felt the blood draining out of her. She clutched the door handle and hung on to it. 'I—I thought you weren't coming until tomorrow,' she stammered.

He stood there looking at her, not saying anything. He looked tired, there were dark shadows under his eyes, and standing there he seemed to fill the cottage doorway.

Tessa swallowed hard. 'Won't you come in?'

He smiled faintly. 'I thought you'd never ask,' he said, and followed her into the living-room.

She waved towards a chair. 'You've come down by train? Did you have a good journey?' she gabbled. Of course he had come by train, that taxi hadn't brought him all the way from London. She looked round the small room rather helplessly. 'I'm afraid I haven't anything much to offer you to drink. Barney likes beer, so I stocked up with that while I was cooking suppers for him, and——' She went across to the built-in cupboard and opened the door. 'Orange juice, lime juice, bitter lemon——'

He sank into a chair. 'Beer will do fine,' he said, and Tessa went into the kitchen and came back with glasses and a can of beer from the fridge. She poured herself some orange juice and sat down in the corner of the sofa.

Alaric took a long swig of beer and put down his glass. 'That's rather good,' he said. 'I think I might quite take to beer.' He studied her face. 'How are you, Tessa? You look pale—have you been working too hard?'

She managed to laugh. 'Of course not. My parents drove over from Devon to visit me one afternoon and I've been to the lab once or twice but there's nothing I can do there yet. It's all looking very smart; you'll be pleased with it, I'm sure.' She rattled on, her voice three tones higher than usual. 'I've been helping Mona quite a bit until she went back into hospital. You knew she'd had her baby—a little girl—isn't that lovely?'

His eyes never left her face. '*You're* lovely,' he said quietly. 'Have you missed me?'

'I've—thought about you,' she said cautiously.

'Nasty thoughts?'

She felt herself flushing. 'I don't have to answer that.'

'You'd be justified,' he said. 'I've had many nasty thoughts about myself recently. That last evening we were at the house together—I behaved badly—I should have known better.'

'I wasn't blameless myself,' Tessa said, flushing painfully, and twisting her fingers together on her lap.

It was a very small parlour; the space between the chair and sofa was narrow. Alaric leaned over and covered both Tessa's hands with one of his. 'Let's not hold a post-mortem,' he said. 'Let's start again where we left off before——' he grinned suddenly '—before sex reared its ugly head. Not,' he added, 'that ugly is a word I would use myself in that connection, but let that pass for the moment. Shall we be friends again, Tessa? I wanted to see you again to try and put things right. I've been very concerned about the way we parted.'

She drew her hands away. Concerned, have you indeed? *I've* been sick at heart. Wretched, despairing, desperate. But he wouldn't be interested in emotional language like that. Men didn't like women who over-reacted, did they?

'Shall we be friends?' he asked again.

'Of course,' she said. 'I'd like that.'

His eyes moved over her face slowly. Then his mouth drew into a wide smile. 'Well, that's good. You've set my mind at rest.'

Nice for you, she thought. I wish my mind were at rest.

He sat back in his chair. 'Well, how's everything? How's the lab progressing? I've rung Barney once or twice for a progress report, but I've been away from London so I haven't always had an opportunity to get in touch.'

'Abroad?' Tessa enquired. If he had been away then he probably wouldn't have been with Cara Everett, and that was a nice thought.

He shook his head. 'No—up in the Midlands. My mama has been pulling off one of her crafty little takeovers. Ferris Knight—your old stamping ground, wasn't it, Tessa?'

She stared at him stupidly. She could feel the blood draining out of her cheeks. Alaric's face began to blur. She *wasn't* going to faint, she wouldn't let herself. She dug her nails into her palms, willing herself with desperation to hold on to her composure. 'Oh, yes, it seems a long time ago.' Her mouth felt stiff but her voice sounded fairly normal. 'How did you find them all up there?'

'Oh fine, fine. I got on pretty well with the management team. They seem a very decent lot—I hadn't met any of them before. I think they'll fit in well with us.'

Had he mentioned her name to the Ferris Knight directors? What was the chance that he had said, 'You remember Tessa Durant—she used to work for you in the lab here, I believe. I'm putting her in a research team that I'm just setting up.' He might even make a joke of it on the 'your loss is my gain' lines.

She looked into his face and saw nothing there but the mildest interest in Ferris Knight and the takeover. He would have gone up to Birmingham to discuss facts and figures at the highest level, not to talk about an unimportant assistant chemist who had left many months ago. And if he *had* mentioned her, would they remember her and the circumstances under which she left the company?

But the risk that he would find out had got closer so that it seemed to hover over her like a threatening black cloud. One day the storm might break and then she would be drowned in the deluge that must follow. Deceit was something that Alaric would never forgive.

She must tell him—now. Her stomach was hollow and her heart was fluttering against her ribs. 'Alaric, there's something——' she began at the exact moment that he said, 'There's a very——'

They both stopped. 'You first,' Alaric said with a grin and Tessa said 'No—you.'

He started again. 'There's a very tempting and savoury smell coming from the kitchen—makes me feel like a Bisto kid. I hadn't time for any lunch. Do you think——?' He put on a pathetic face.

'Of course,' Tessa said, getting to her feet immediately. A short reprieve—and perhaps he would be in a mellow mood when he had enjoyed a meal. Wasn't that supposed to be the right way to approach a man with some unpleasant news?

She opened the oven door and prodded the steak in the casserole. Beautifully tender. And the carrots made a nice splash of colour in the rich dark gravy. She popped a handful of frozen peas in to complete the colour scheme and put the dish back in the oven. By the time she had set the table it would all be ready.

Her hands were shaking as she gathered mats and cutlery and went back into the living-room. Alaric had moved to the sofa and was lying with his feet up, his eyes closed. He really did look desperately tired.

He didn't open his eyes as she set table-mats for three, placing knives and forks and spoons down one at a time, careful not to make a sound. Tiptoeing back to the kitchen she cut brown bread in small hunks and arranged it on a plate, set out butter and cheese and a bowl of apples. She didn't suppose Barney would arrive yet; he always stayed with Mona until the very end of visiting-time. It wouldn't do the casserole any harm to remain in the oven for another half-hour—or another hour, for that matter.

She went back into the living-room and lowered herself cautiously into a chair. Alaric was fast asleep now and she sat watching him, seeing the little lines on his face smoothed out, the long dark lashes resting on his cheekbones, his mouth relaxed as he breathed evenly and quietly.

Looking at him, at his long body stretched out on the sofa, his feet propped up on the arm-rest, her eyes were misty and her heart twisted with love and tenderness, and regret for what had happened between them on the night before he left for London. It was cruel that the memory of Marc should have suddenly reared up with such frightening intensity, almost as if he had come back to spoil her hopes of happiness. But of course that was stupid thinking. Marc couldn't harm her now—not if she told Alaric about the Ferris Knight affair. She would tell him everything, exactly as it happened; suggest that he should contact Tom Jarvis, who would certainly back up her story and confirm her innocence.

Yes, that was what she would do, and having made up her mind it was as if a great load had fallen from her shoulders. She smiled as she remembered that Libra people were supposed to have difficulty making up their minds. This time, she resolved, she would make a firm decision and stick to it.

She would tell him tonight if there was an opportunity, or if not she would make a point of seeing him early tomorrow morning at the lab and asking for an interview in a businesslike way. Because after all, she argued with herself, it *was* a business matter.

Perhaps it would be better if she did leave it until tomorrow morning in any case. He really looked too tired tonight to listen to her rather complicated story.

He opened his eyes and smiled at her and her heart turned over. 'Mouse,' he said. 'As quiet as a little mouse. How long have you been sitting there?'

'Only a few minutes,' she said brightly. She didn't want him to think that she had been sitting there gazing at him. They were friends; that was what he wanted and that was a start. If he guessed that she was in love with him it was going to spoil everything. 'Barney should be here soon, but we can start our supper now if you're really starving.'

He slewed his legs round and sat up. 'Oh, I'm starving, no doubt about that. Ravenous.' The calculated laziness of his voice, the way he was looking at her, told her beyond doubt that he wasn't referring to the supper.

Tessa looked away quickly, her cheeks warm. 'I'll go and take the casserole out of the oven then.' As she disappeared into the kitchen she thought she heard a faint chuckle following her.

Anger bubbled inside her as she pulled on her oven gloves. How *could* he? Surely, after all that had happened between them, he didn't need to treat her as if she were a giggly teenager? She carried the casserole dish to the table and said in a formal, hostessy voice, 'Would you care to wash? The bathroom's through there on the left.'

'Thanks,' he said, getting to his feet.

The room was tiny and Tessa pulled herself back against the table to give him room to pass—and so that he wouldn't touch her. But he paused, putting out a hand to tip up her chin and force her to meet his eyes.

'I'm glad we're friends again, Tessa,' he said quietly, and there was something in his voice that made her heart beat unevenly. He had changed towards her in the time he had been away, she sensed that, but she couldn't say how. A moment ago he had been trying to bait her, to make her blush, but now there was a deeper note in his voice that disturbed her at a much more basic level. Or perhaps she was just imagining it?

Barney arrived, hugging a bottle of wine, before she could give the matter any more thought. 'Something to celebrate,' he announced, ducking his head to avoid the lintel of the front door. He dumped the bottle on the table. 'I've just heard that Tessa has put on two ounces today. How about that then? Oh, hello, Alaric, you here?' as Alaric appeared from the back of the cottage.

Barney looked faintly embarrassed, and it seemed as if he might be going to make some excuse and leave again, but Tessa moved quickly behind him and closed the front door. Barney was a sensitive man, as she had discovered, and he must not be allowed to think he was butting in on anything.

Alaric came forward holding out his hand. 'Congratulations, Barney, once again. In person this time. How does it feel to be a father?'

'Great,' Barney said. 'Just great.' He glanced at the casserole, steaming on the table. 'Now, I'll leave you two to——'

Tessa moved to the table, pretending not to hear, saying, 'We were going to wait supper for you, Barney, only greedy Alaric said he was starving.' She threw a nasty look at Alaric, to which he responded with a wide grin. 'Come on, let's sit down and eat before my work of art gets cold. I'll get a bottle-opener.'

Barney, apparently reassured that he was expected when he noticed the third place set at the table, drew the cork from the bottle of wine and filled three glasses. Alaric said, 'What exactly are we celebrating? You said Tessa had gained two ounces.' The smokey-grey eyes danced as he looked Tessa up and down across the table. 'I know she's a slim girl, but two ounces surely isn't all that critical?'

Barney and Tessa burst out laughing. Barney said, 'Of course, you wouldn't know, we've called the baby Tessa. And if she turns out as sweet and kind and lovely as this Tessa——' he raised his glass gallantly '—we won't have anything to complain about. Let's drink to both Tessas.'

Alaric raised his glass. 'To both Tessas,' he said, and again there was that new look in his eyes as they met hers steadily over the rim of his glass, and she looked away, confused.

But after that the meal was a light-hearted occasion. Things were going well. A new baby, a new laboratory,   both matters for rejoicing, as Alaric said, refilling their glasses. Tessa was beginning to feel warm and relaxed. She wondered what would happen when they had had coffee—would Barney discreetly leave, as seemed likely? And if she was left alone with Alaric, would she feel equal to launching into her unhappy story and explanation?

In the end, the decision was taken out of her hands. The two men decided to drive over to the laboratory together. Barney seemed slightly worried about a new microscope which hadn't been delivered.

'I'll go and get your Jag out of the garage, and follow you over in the Escort,' Barney said, disappearing into the darkness round the side of the cottage.

Alaric and Tessa were left standing together in the doorway, and the warm summer-evening smells of grasses and plants were all around them. He put a hand on her shoulder. 'You'll be coming over to the lab with Barney in the morning? There are things I want to discuss with you.'

She nodded. 'Yes, of course. I want to know what my duties are going to be.'

She heard his low chuckle. 'I shan't leave you in any doubt about that,' he said, 'I intend——' The rest of the sentence was drowned in the noise of the powerful engine of the Jaguar as it appeared from the garage and pulled up at the end of the short front path. 'Goodnight, sweet Tess,' Alaric whispered close to her ear and planted a kiss just below it. 'I'll see you in the morning.' Then he slid into the Jaguar's driving-seat as Barney got out of it, and with a lift of his hand in salute, roared away down the lane.

Tessa's cottage had no garage, and Barney's Ford Escort was parked on the grass verge on the far side of the lane. 'I'll pick you up in the morning about nine,' he shouted as he got into the car and Tessa called back,

'OK.'

She stood in the doorway until the sound of both cars had faded away. Then she turned and went slowly inside and stood leaning her back against the closed door.

It might have been imagination—or wishful thinking—that gave her the idea that Alaric's approach to her had changed. She mustn't build on what had probably been a genuine wish to put something right that had gone wrong between himself and one of his new employees. And he had always—except for that one occasion when his masculine sexual drive had got the better of him—adopted a light approach towards her, something between irony and teasing. No, she mustn't let herself get carried away into hoping.

But hope isn't easily destroyed by an application of common sense. And Tessa went to bed that night with a feeling that something new and wonderful might be just below the horizon for her, as new and wonderful as a new day's sunrise.

CHAPTER SEVEN

TESSA wakened on Friday morning still with the same feeling that something wonderful had happened. She stretched luxuriously, remembering what it was. Alaric was here—only a mile or less away—and she would see him this morning. 'I'll see you in the morning,' he had said, and he'd kissed her. She put her hand on the place—just below her left ear—and a surge of desire ran through her.

This wouldn't do at all, she told herself firmly, sliding out of bed and padding downstairs to the bathroom. Friendship was the name of the game at present. That was what he had asked for and that was what she had to offer. Definitely no lovemaking, for the simple reason that there was definitely no love—not on his side.

The water hadn't heated up properly yet, and she gasped as she stepped under the shower. 'Definitely no love,' she told herself again, aloud. He had never given her any reason to suppose that he was in love with her. Gratitude—yes. Friendliness—yes. Physical desire—oh, yes indeed. Tessa stepped from under the shower and towelled herself down vigorously.

Just ordinary male lust, that was what he had demonstrated on that last evening before he left for London, wasn't it? *Wasn't* it? Born of—what did they

141

call it?—proximity. It would be as well, she decided, to make sure there wasn't any proximity in the future. She knew only too well how close she had been to disaster on that night. Because it would have been a disaster to give way to her own hunger and start a relationship that would have led to nothing but misery at the end. She had been saved only by that sudden black memory of Marc coming out of the past to warn and terrify her. Saved at the cost of wounding Alaric's male ego! How furious he had been with her, she remembered with a shiver. Well, anyway she would be careful not to get into a situation like that again. There had to be love on *both* sides, she repeated to herself; nothing less would do.

She wasn't sure that she had believed Cara Everett's nasty suggestions that Alaric had arranged to have her—Tessa—here so that she would be 'available' when he visited the lab. That sounded more like the fabrication of a jealous woman than a motive that she could ascribe to Alaric. But there seemed little doubt, from what she had heard from Freda Fowkes, and from the way that Cara had breezed into the bedroom on that fatal morning, that there was something between Cara Everett and Alaric. Tessa didn't want to dwell on that.

Back upstairs in the bedroom, she dressed in a businesslike white blouse and denim skirt and went to the window. The bedroom, like the sitting-room, overlooked the grassy land behind which a line of hills rose up to cut across the sky. Tessa loved this view of the hills, with the little groups of sheep moving slowly around as they grazed, and the wide expanse of sky at the top. Sometimes, on a breezy, sunny day, cloud-shadows would chase each other across the hills, but this morning a faint haze lay over everything, blotting out sky and sheep and signalling the start of another hot summer day. Tessa sighed with pleasure. She was so lucky, she told herself firmly. She would just enjoy being here and looking forward to a new, interesting job, and stop allowing herself to feel lovesick.

As she moved away from the window she heard the noise of a car below and looked down to see Barney's Escort back out of his garage, reverse across the lane and drive away quickly. Tessa consulted her watch on the dressing-table. Not yet eight o'clock—where was he going? What had happened? He surely wouldn't be leaving for the lab so early, and anyway he had arranged to give her a lift this morning and he couldn't have forgotten, could he?

An emergency at the hospital? Oh surely not—not when everything seemed to be going so well yesterday. Tessa wouldn't let herself consider that. It must be something that had turned up at the lab—or, most likely, *not* turned up. Something to do with the missing microscope, perhaps. They had had difficulties with deliveries and Alaric had probably phoned an SOS to Barney. Yes, that would be it, she reassured herself as she went down to make toast and coffee for her breakfast. Barney would remember her and come back, and if not, she would walk over to the lab; that would be no hardship on a beautiful morning.

By nine o'clock she had finished breakfast and washed up and when Barney hadn't put in an appearance she went upstairs to put on a pair of low-heeled sandals suitable for walking along the lanes. Opening the wardrobe cupboard she looked dubiously at the meagre supply of clothes hanging there. She would have to do something about getting her things from London soon, and decide whether or not to give notice on her flat. Alaric hadn't mentioned a rent for the cottage, and she wondered if it went with the job. She would have to ask him. If so, it might be a good idea to keep on the London flat for a while, until she was quite sure that things were going to work out here.

But more urgently, what was she going to wear for the party at the lab this evening? She supposed the sensible thing would be to wear the yellow seersucker dress—the one she had bought for her holiday with Marc, the holiday that hadn't happened.

She held up the dress, frowning. She couldn't—she simply *couldn't* wear it tonight for the opening of the lab—Alaric's great occasion. She herself would play only a very minor role in that occasion, of course, and even if he noticed the dress she was wearing it wouldn't mean a thing to him. but it would to her. She would look at the dress and remember—no, she couldn't wear it. She clattered the hanger back on the rail and pushed it away to the far end. The dress could go to Oxfam and be worn with pleasure by some girl who didn't have any bitter memories clinging to it.

There was the sound of a car pulling up outside the cottage and she picked up her handbag and ran downstairs. 'Hello, Barney,' she sang out as she slammed the front door behind her, 'I thought you'd forgotten——'

But it wasn't Barney getting out of his Escort. It was Alaric, with the Jaguar panting gently behind him like its jungle namesake. He came up the path towards her and her heart flipped painfully because he looked so stunningly attractive in jeans and an open-neck check shirt, his brown hair damp and brushed back casually.

They met in the middle of the path and he stopped and looked down at her with an odd expression. 'Hello, Tessa,' he said. 'Good morning.'

'Good morning,' she said, with a mortifying catch in her voice, and then chattered on nervously. 'I thought it was Barney—I saw him go out very early and I was a bit worried in case there'd been a crisis at the hospital——'

He hadn't moved. His smoke-grey eyes were still studying her face. Then he gave a slight start. 'Crisis? Oh—Barney. No, no crisis. He was wanted early at the lab, that's all, so I came instead. I have to drive into Poole first, to pick up some gear that's waiting at the station there, so I thought I'd take you along with me for the ride. There isn't anything particular for you to do at the lab yet. The caterers have moved in and Mrs Measures is keeping a motherly eye on them. Like to come with me?'

Just a casual invitation, and she answered as casually as she knew how, 'Thanks, that would be nice,' ignoring the trembly feeling that his presence was producing somewhere behind her ribs. 'Would there be any big shops in Poole? I'd like to have a look for a dress to wear at the party this evening. I only came for an overnight stay, if you remember, and I'm woefully short of clothes.

He opened the door of the Jaguar and she got in, squeezing herself as far into the corner of the passenger seat as possible so that she wouldn't have to touch him while he was driving. When he had taken his place behind the wheel he said, 'Shops? Oh yes. There's Beales—quite a large store, I'm sure you'll find something there. You don't know Poole?' he added conversationally as the car moved off along the lane.

Tessa shook her head. 'This is a new part of the country to me.' Her voice had suddenly become squeaky. It seemed impossible to be natural with this man sitting so close beside her.

They had stopped at the turning on the main road and he glanced over to her corner with a smile.

'I shall look forward to showing it to you,' he said and his eyes held hers for a moment before they turned back to the road as he waited for a gap in the traffic. Tessa stared out of the side window, her heart racing. She should never have come with him, she thought; even sitting here beside him in a car, having a perfectly ordinary conversation, left her feeling tense and churned up inside.

Without looking round Alaric reached out and put a hand on her arm. 'Relax, lovie,' he said quietly. 'We're friends, remember? Let's just enjoy the lovely summer day together. Yes?'

It was as if he had touched a sensitive spot that suddenly released all her tensions. It seemed ridiculous to keep up a kind of cold war between them. And another thing—if he guessed that she had fallen in love with him—that that was the reason for her awkwardness with him—she would want to curl up and die.

'Yes,' she said a little shakily. 'You're right. Look, the mist's clearing and the sun's coming out.'

Their way took them through a tiny village and a little later they stopped to pay at a toll-gate. Then they were out on an open road with a wide expanse of the heath on both sides. The gorse was still golden at the side of the road and tufts of purple, dotted here and there on the grassy hummocks, promised a second flowering of heather later in the year. Alaric pressed a button to slide back the roof of the car. The mist had cleared completely now and the sun was warm on their heads and their bare arms.

Tessa drew in a long breath of pleasure. She felt young and ridiculously happy, like a child at a party. She wanted to dance and sing and pat coloured balloons and eat jelly and trifle, with no grown-up fears about what tomorrow would bring. This is my lovely day, she thought, and everything was fun because Alaric was here and she could turn her head and look at him and see him smile back at her. The clanking chain-ferry that took them across the harbour entrance, with the waves lapping almost on to the car wheels as the Jaguar wedged itself in among all the other cars, was a new experience, and that was fun too.

'Look at that seagull.' Tessa pointed to a huge gull who was having a free ride, perching proudly on one of the front rails as the ferry chugged across the narrow stretch of water. 'He thinks he's a noble figurehead on the prow of a Viking ship.'

'Not a bit of it,' Alaric chuckled. 'He's here for the free lunch. Look!'

Tessa looked and saw that foot-passengers on the side decks were throwing bits of bread up in the air to be neatly caught by the gull.

'Is there no romance left in the world?' she sighed.

'Lots, so long as you know where to look for it.' Alaric chuckled again and rubbed his cheek against her hair. And Tessa didn't even fight against the thrill that ran through her like a lightning flash. It was all part of her lovely day.

Once off the ferry the scenery changed quite dramatically. The open stretches of heath were left behind and tall blocks of flats and hotels lined one side of a smooth, wide road that swept round a broad expanse of water. The reds and yellows of sailboards skimmed across its surface, or wobbled precariously to keel over and provide their navigators with a dip in the choppy blue water.

'Is it a lake?' Tessa asked, but Alaric told her it was part of Poole Harbour.

'It's all a bit too civilised for me around here,' he remarked, keeping his eyes dutifully ahead as the long queue of cars moved at a dignified pace towards the town centre.

'You're a wild man of the wild heath?' she teased, and it was lovely that, for a change, it was her turn to tease *him*, without feeling self-conscious. It might be wishful thinking, but she felt a new closeness between them, as if she could say anything to him.

'Precisely,' he grinned. 'And I'm not at all looking forward to being based in London again after all the months of freedom down here.'

So he wasn't yearning to get back to Cara? Tessa felt a small glow of satisfaction.

'This place will be choc-a-bloc with visitors in a few weeks,' he went on. 'In August you have to queue for an hour or more to get across the ferry. But today it should be reasonably possible to move around in the town. We'll park the car and you can buy your dress before I pick up my parcel at the station. We might take a stroll down to the old quay, it's quite fascinating, and then we could get a bite of lunch before we go back. How does that appeal?'

'Sounds fine,' Tessa said and added politely, 'if you can spare the time.'

He still kept his attention on the traffic straight ahead, but it was as if he looked deep into her eyes as he said in a voice that reached down into the centre of her being, 'I can't think of any way I'd rather spend the time than with you, my dearest.'

Tessa was struck dumb. *My dearest!* The words had come out so easily, so naturally. And somehow they were more intimate than the usual 'darling' or 'sweetheart'. 'Dearest' seemed to imply a closeness, an understanding that would stretch ahead into the future. Almost as if they were already lovers.

She swallowed with difficulty because her throat seemed to have closed up. But she managed, somehow, to quip, 'Well now, that sure is a pretty speech, Mr Brent.'

'It should be,' he said, not smiling at all. 'It came

from the heart.'

At that moment they turned off the road into the entrance to the multi-story car park, and Alaric had to apply all his attention to guiding the big car through the dark, snaky twists and turns that led up to Floor D.

'Now for your dress,' he said, locking the car. 'You won't have far to go—I seem to remember that Beale's ladies' dress department is on this level. Come along, I'll show you.' He led the way across a bridge over a side road and into what was evidently a very large covered shopping arcade, teeming with people.

Holding her arm he guided her through the crowd. 'Poole is very proud of its Arndale Centre,' he told her. 'All very modern, and it's revolutionised shopping in the town. I remember when there were only the small High Street shops—my grandmother used to bring me here sometimes—but now we've got the lot—Boots, Tesco's Sainsbury's, Marks and Sparks, everything you could think of.'

'I could get my dress at Marks and Sparks,' Tessa said, thinking of her bank account. 'I usually do.'

'Well—ye-es,' Alaric conceded, 'you probably could, but let's go to Beale's. It won't be so crowded, and you can browse there to your heart's content.'

He was right about the ladies' dress department, it was on the higher floor of the store and they walked straight into it at car-park level. 'Very clever,' Tessa murmured, wondering how Alaric came to know quite so much about buying ladies' clothes. Perhaps he had brought Cara here, she thought, on one of her 'little trips' into Dorset when Alaric was stationed

here. Jealousy pricked like a sharp needle and she
opened her mouth to insist on finding another shop,
but by that time they were walking on soft carpet with
rails of eye-catching clothes all around, so at least she
had to pretend to be interested.

She stopped at a stand of blue dresses, simple shirt-
waister styles with front buttonings and turned-back
revered collars. One of these would do very well. As a
mere assistant chemist in the new department, the last
thing she wanted was to dress up and look as if she
were trying to draw attention to herself. She took a
blue dress off the rail and held it up. Beside her,
Alaric shook his head. 'No,' he said definitely.

Tessa raised her eyebrows. 'Didn't you want to go
to the station to collect a parcel?' she said pointedly.
'We could meet somewhere——'

He grinned. 'Not on your life. I'm not missing the
fun of watching a pretty girl choose a dress.'

A sales-lady was approaching. 'May we see
something in your model range?' Alaric enquired
before Tessa could say a word. 'Green, for
preference.'

'Certainly, sir.' The woman almost appeared to
melt before his smile. 'If you'll come this way, please.'

He put a hand at Tessa's elbow but she shook it off.
'I really prefer to choose myself. And I never wear
green.' Not only was he being abominably high-
handed, but he would probably talk her into buying
something she couldn't afford.

'No?' he smiled maddeningly. 'You should. Hasn't
anyone told you that your eyes are the colour of
emeralds?'

'Go away,' she told him.

But he said nothing and stayed beside her as the assistant led them to a series of glass-fronted cases in a far corner of the department. She slid back one of the doors and turned to size Tessa up. 'A perfect twelve,' she murmured but she wasn't addressing Tessa, she was smiling at the man beside her, and he nodded smugly. As if, Tessa thought indignantly, someone had admired his taste in thoroughbred mares or vintage wine.

The assistant had taken down two apple-green chiffon dresses from the selection inside the case, but Alaric shook his head immediately. 'Too fussy,' he said. 'Something more—er—close-fitting, we had in mind, didn't we, darling?' He beamed at Tessa who glared back at him as the woman turned away again.

When I get out of here, Tessa resolved, fuming, I shall go straight back to the cottage. There must be a bus or something that I could catch. And I am not—definitely *not*—going to buy one of these pricey little numbers hanging up here.

'Now that,' she heard Alaric saying, 'is more like it.'

The assistant was holding up a dress, and if there was such a thing as love at first sight as applied to dresses, Tessa had to admit that this was it. In soft cotton, the skirt had broad stripes of emerald and white, gathered into a narrow waist. The top was of plain emerald, slash-necked, with short white-cuffed sleeves and a white kid belt that fastened over the tiny pleats at the waistline of the skirt. As the assistant turned it on its hanger the dress promised a miracle of swinging, clinging femininity. It also looked hideously expensive.

'Try it on,' Alaric said lazily.

The sales-lady was pulling back the curtain of a fitting-booth and somehow Tessa found herself and the dress inside. She searched for a price label and winced at the figure on it. She certainly wasn't going to be bullied by Alaric Brent into spending that much money on one dress. He was probably used to choosing dresses for Cara Everett and she, no doubt, drew five times the salary that Tessa could expect. Goodness, she could buy a super winter coat for that amount. Anyway, the dress probably wouldn't fit, she assured herself, pulling off the white blouse and denim skirt.

The dress fitted like a dream. Tessa drew in a long breath as she stared at herself in the mirror and had to admit she had never looked like this before. Alaric was right, damn the man, green did do something for her, and the top moulded her softly in all the right places. She lifted her mane of silky dark hair and let it fall forward on her cheeks, then she twisted and turned before the mirror and the skirt swished round her long, slim legs. Would Cara Everett be at the party, she wondered. That thought decided her. She stepped outside to where Alaric was lolling casually on a gilt chair that looked too frail to support his weight.

'Yes,' he said, nodding judicially, and again there was that odd expression in his eyes. 'Yes, that's the one. You like it?'

She wasn't going to rave about the dress, nor admit that the price appalled her. Fortunately she was nowhere near up to the limit on her credit card. 'I think it will do quite well,' she said coolly, and smiled at the sales-lady who was returning, ready to enthuse.

Back in the fitting booth, she looked in the mirror and sighed. 'You come in determined not to buy the dress and go out wondering how you're going to pay for it. Why do you have to dither? *Why* were you born in Libra?'

'Wasn't I right?' Alaric demanded as Tessa tucked her credit card away and received the large carrier bag. 'I thought you'd get something nice here. I know the place well—I brought Mrs Measures and her daughter here a couple of times in the spring. The daughter was choosing a wedding outfit.'

So it wasn't Cara Everett he came shopping with! Suddenly all the colours around looked brighter, and she was glad she had overspent on the dress, because he thought she looked good in it. She smiled sweetly over her shoulder at him as the escalator carried them downwards. 'I'm sure you're *always* right,' she teased.

'I've had another clever idea,' he said when they reached the ground floor. 'I think I've had enough of town already. I'll collect my parcel at the station and then why don't we buy some sandwiches and drive back over the ferry and have a picnic on the heath before we go back to the lab?'

'Oh *yes*,' Tessa agreed. 'But—shouldn't I be there to help Mrs Measures with the preparations for this evening?'

'No need. Mrs Measures has everything in hand with the caterers.' He smiled down at her, linking his arm with hers as they went out into the big, crowded hall of the shopping-centre. 'All you will have to do is walk in looking beautiful.'

Her green eyes sparkled up at him. 'No problem,' she grinned back. 'Let's go to Marks and Sparks on the way to the station. They make gorgeous prawn sandwiches.'

Oh, this was turning out a really wonderful day.

'That,' said Alaric, lying back against a hummock of bristly grass, hands linked behind his head, 'was an excellent lunch. You were right about the prawn sandwiches.'

Tessa stuffed pieces of cling film and an empty bottle of Perrier water back into a plastic carrier bag.

'And you were right about the heath. It's the kind of place that grows on you. We're only about fifty yards from the car and the road, and yet we might be in another world.'

She was beginning to understand his love for this place. It was so vast and empty at first sight, and yet somehow it seemed to contain ancient, secret things from a long-ago past. She was sure it was full of history. Perhaps, millions of years ago, gigantic dinosaurs had plodded in the undergrowth here. Looking down she saw a small beetle-like creature scurrying away into a clump of dried heather and laughed.

At the sound Alaric opened his eyes and smiled at her under his dark lashes. He looked the picture of contentment. He was happy with her, she thought, and again there was this new feeling of closeness.

'And what have you been doing with yourself while I haven't been here to keep an eye on you?' he said.

Tessa sat hugging her knees. 'Enjoying myself, mostly. I was brave enough to have one or two swims. The water wasn't too cold. I've cooked and shopped and spent the rest of my time with Mona—the doctors insisted on bed-rest for her until she went back into hospital to have the baby. So I was doing my Florence Nightingale act again. I'm beginning to think I missed my vocation when I became a chemist.'

'Why did you?' he asked lazily. 'Become a chemist, I mean.'

She glanced quickly at him, catching her breath. This conversation might lead into dangerous channels. Last night she had made up her mind to tell him all about the Ferris Knight affair, but not now—she couldn't risk spoiling her lovely day.

'I couldn't decide between chemistry and history and my careers mistress at school guided me towards the science side.' She laughed lightly. 'I'm a Libra, you know, and Libras have difficulty making decisions.' That should change the subject, she thought.

'I know all about that, my married sister is a Libra too. Getting her to make up her mind about anything is a major undertaking. But she insists that Libra ladies are always very beautiful so I have to forgive her. She has a point, Tessa,' he added softly, 'and you're living proof of it, my sweet.'

'Flattery!' she laughed but he shook his head and said firmly,

'The truth.'

There was a silence, broken only by the twittering of larks, high above and out of sight, and the distant hum of cars on the road across the heath. Alaric lay back comfortably, eyes closed again, and it took all Tessa's self-control to stop herself lying down beside him. That wouldn't do at all, because it might be misconstrued. And she mustn't go on analysing his words, reading more into them than he intended, seeing more in his eyes than friendship.

But as she looked down at his sun-tanned face she suddenly wanted urgently to touch him, to trace the faint lines that ran across his forehead, to stroke back the thick brown hair where it grew at his temples. She had a strong, wicked need to bend down and lay her lips against the faintly sensual line of his mouth, and the idea sent a pulsing ache thorugh her. Stop it, she told herself, oh, stop it, you fool.

He opened his eyes, but only a little way, so that the long dark lashes almost hid them. 'Why don't you?' he said softly.

'Why don't I w-what?' she stammered.

'Do what you were thinking about.'

He reached up and pulled her down to him, and there was no way she was going to resist. 'You were thinking you'd like to be kissed, weren't you? Go on, admit it.' The smoky-grey eyes teased her.

Keep it light, Tessa. Whatever you do, don't get emotional. 'Well,' she drawled, 'I'm only human and you, Mr Brent, are quite an attractive specimen of manhood.'

He propped himself on his elbows. 'Is that all?' His face was very close and it was getting closer and closer as she lay on her back looking up into it. 'Merely "attractive"? Not magnetic—dynamic?' His teeth were creamy-white against the brown of his cheeks as he laughed down at her. 'Not sexy, seductive, irresistible?' His face was only inches away now. 'Go on, admit it.'

'OK, OK,' she gasped weakly, 'I admit it all,' and closed her eyes as his mouth touched hers.

Thinking about it later, she decided that he hadn't intended the kiss to develop the way it did. At first he brushed his lips lightly against hers, his hands holding her shoulders easily. Then he planted small kisses up the side of her nose and along her forehead, smoothing her dark hair back with one hand and balancing his weight on the other.

Tessa lay quiet, savouring the pleasure he was giving her, soft and warm, content to accept the little teasing kisses that he placed gently on her cheeks and her closed eyes. This was just a flirtation, nothing more—almost it was like the experiments of one's schooldays.

Then everything changed. She could feel the sudden surge of passion in him, the hardening and tensing of his body as he drew her against him. His mouth closed on hers in urgent demand, and her mouth answered as her back arched spontaneously and she pressed herself against the length of him. Her arms went round him, clinging into his waist, his hips, as they moved together in a sudden frenzy.

Then, with dazed disbelief, she heard him groan, 'Oh God, Tessa, not now,' and he dragged himself away from her, got to his feet and stood with his back to her.

Tessa sat up, pushing her hair away from her face, close to tears and struggling against disappointment and humiliation that was like a blow to the stomach. She looked at his straight back as he stood staring across the heath, brown hair lifting in the breeze, and thought that she would never understand him—never.

Then he turned and came back to her. 'Playing with fire,' he said, smiling ruefully. 'Nanny always warned me against that. Sorry, Tessa, things got a little out of hand.' So he could even make a joke of a moment like that, could he?

Tessa picked up the plastic carrier, and her handbag. 'We'd better get back, hadn't we?' she said, and walked in front of him to the car.

The short drive to the laboratory was accomplished in silence and ten minutes later the Jaguar drew up in front of the old grey building.

Cara Everett was standing at the top of the steps, wearing bright red trousers and a canary-yellow shirt. Alaric switched off the engine and got out of the car as she came running down the steps to him.

'I got your message this morning, darling, and I came straight away. Your mama is driving down later.' She put her arms around Alaric's neck and kissed him. If she had noticed Tessa still sitting in the passenger seat, she showed no sign of it.

She linked her arm in Alaric's and pulled him towards the steps. 'Let's go up to your office, I've got lots to tell you.'

Barney appeared then from round the back of the house, and Alaric detached himself from Cara and opened the back door of the Jaguar. The parcel he had collected at the station was on the seat and beside the parcel was the carrier bag containing Tessa's dress.

He hesistated for a moment, frowning. Then he looked towards Barney. 'Your parcel's there, Barney,' he said, 'and could you spare a minute or two to run Tessa back to her cottage? I've got a few things to discuss with Cara. Take the Jag, if you like.'

'Sure, boss. Will do.' Barney slid willingly behind the wheel of the big car and Alaric stood beside the window, staring moodily at Tessa, who hadn't moved from the passenger seat. The car backed round and drew away and as it went she saw Alaric join Cara. The picture was very clear in the sunshine. The big, smiling girl in the brilliantly coloured outfit against the grey stone of the old house, holding out her hand to Alaric as he climbed the steps towards her.

Tessa let out her breath. She took back what she had thought about not understanding Alaric. It now seemed painfully clear why he hadn't wanted to linger any longer on the heath—with her.

CHAPTER EIGHT

BARNEY chatted away happily on the drive back to the cottage. 'Amazing how everything comes together in the end. Only yesterday we were short of that microscope and I can tell you I was relieved, this morning, when a message came through early that it had turned up at Poole Station. I think the chairman—or should it be chairperson?—Mrs Brent, I mean, will be impressed. I hope so. Alaric hasn't actually said much about it, but I think he's had a fight on his hads to get the lab established. Of course, it won't be a financial asset to the company for years, if ever. Research has to be funded—but Brent's are a flourishing firm—they can afford it. And if we do have a spectacular breakthrough there's no knowing where we shall go from there. Public interest in more natural medicine seems to be on the up and up.'

Tessa listened with only half an ear, and when they reached the cottage she took her dress-carrier from the back seat, smiling at Barney absently. 'Thanks for the lift, Barney. See you later at the party, what a pity Mona can't be there.' Oh, if only she didn't have to go to the party and see Cara Everett hanging possessively on Alaric's arm!

Barney's mouth softened. 'That would have been great, but she says she'll be thinking about us and keeping her fingers crossed. And I've arranged to take Alaric in tomorrow to see her and young Tessa, and we'll be able to tell her all about it. Well, I'll be getting back. What about transport for you, Tessa? Will Alaric be giving you a lift?'

She almost said, No, Cara's arrived and Alaric's ditched me, but she mustn't involve the good-natured Barney in her own troubles. 'I've arranged to come along with the Clarks, next door,' she told him and he nodded and lifted a hand in salute and drove away with a roar.

Of course she hadn't arranged anything with the Clarks, she had thought of nothing but Alaric all day. But that little fantasy was over now, she reminded herself, it had finished the moment Cara Everett ran down the steps to him, so the sooner she got herself back into the real world the better.

Sheila Clark was at home when Tessa rang the bell, and seemed delighted to see her. 'Of course we'll give you a lift. We're taking Dick Foster too, from next door, he's just moved in.'

Sheila was a tall, fairish young woman with untidy hair and a long, clever face. 'You and Dick should get on,' she said. 'It seems you both trained at Birmingham—he's looking forward to meeting you again. He's a very good-looking young man,' she added with a twinkle. 'Come along about six, it'll only take us a few minutes to get to the lab.'

Tessa thanked her and went back to her cottage. The name of Dick Foster didn't register with her, and she had forgotten it the next moment. She looked at her watch and saw that it was nearly four o'clock. She went into the kitchen and made tea. What would we do without tea? she asked herself wryly, just as so many ther unhappy women have done over the years.

For a little while, this morning, she had imagined that something had changed between herself and Alaric, but she had been wrong. Nothing had changed. It had merely been a friendly gesture on his part, to take her along with him on his trip to Poole and show an interest in the dress she was buying. He had teased her, just as he'd done so often. And his kiss—proximity again, nothing more. Just the impulse of the moment, and he hd made sure not to let it go further, hadn't he? He must have guessed that Cara would be waiting for him at the lab. Tessa's cheeks burned with sick humiliation.

There was a knock on the front door and a fair young man in a tweed suit and large spectacles stood there. Tessa's thought had been so far away that for the moment she stared at him blankly.

'Tessa Durant? Don't you remember me? Dick Foster—I was in the year after yours at Birmingham.'

'Of *course*, the told me you were one of the new team—do c ome in, I've just made some tea.'

She settled him in a chair and found some biscuits and poured out tea for them both. 'Do tell me what you've been doing,' she said and listened politely as he gave her a run-down of his career since graduation. It took quite a time and Tessa, afterwards, couldn't have repeated a word of what he said. The smile on her mouth felt as if it were glued on as she put in a word here and there: 'Yes, of course.' 'Well, that was wonderful' and 'You *were* lucky, weren't you? But I seem to remember you were the star student of your year.'

That went down well, and Dick launched forth—after a modest disclaimer—into more details of the various jobs he had had since leaving college.

'But I was just so lucky in the end,' he finished, helping himself to his fourth biscuit, 'to be taken on at Brent's lab in Bristol. It's a super firm to work for—I expect you've found that too, Tessa. And then to be extra lucky and have the chance of coming down here. It seems almost too good to be true. Alaric Brent came to Bristol specially to interview some of us for the job, and you could have knocked me down with the proverbial feather when I heard I'd landed it. He's a great chap, isn't he? Have you come across him?'

'Oh, yes, I've met him several times,' Tessa said. She took a gulp of tea and nearly choked on it.

Dick was off again, glowing with pride and enthusiasm—about the job, about the cottage next door but one, obviously floating high on Cloud Nine. It was nice, Tessa thought, to see someone for whom life was going so well. Perhaps the clue was to concentrate on one's career and forget about relationships. That was what she must do in future. She would enjoy her job here and it would be great to get to know her new colleagues. And eventually the yearning pain that gnawed away inside her would get less, wouldn't it? Just at the moment it seemed to be tearing her apart, and it was nearly impossible to keep the smile fixed on her mouth as Dick went on to say how lucky it was to meet her again here, and how they must get together soon and find out all the places to visit.

'Oh, yes, that would be nice,' Tessa said.

She saw Dick glance at her, frowning a little. He must have sensed her lack of attention and she added quickly, not wanting to hurt his feelings, 'Yes, we must do that, there seems to be lots of interesting things to see around here.'

She smiled at him and he beamed back and got up to sit beside her on the sofa. 'We can have some good times together, can't we, Tessa?' He touched her hand rather shyly. 'You know, I so often noticed you, back at the university, but you were in the top league and I didn't dare——'

Both of them spun round as the door opened behind them. Alaric stood there, looking huge in the small room. He took in at a glance the two on the sofa, Dick Foster's hand on Tessa's as he leaned a little towards her.

The boy gathered himself together immediately and jumped to his feet, his fair cheeks flushing.

'Tessa, there are one or two things I want to go through with you before the "do" this evening—if it's convenient.' Alaric's glance flicked over Dick Foster, standing rather awkwardly beside the sofa. He nodded curtly then his smoke-grey eyes met Tessa's again. Gone was the togetherness she thought she had discerned earlier in the day. His expression was coolly businesslike; there was almost a touch of hostility in it.

Dick looked from one to the other of them. 'Well, I'll be off then. I'll see you later,' he muttered, and neither of the other two heard him go.

'I apologise for barging in like that,' Alaric said distantly. 'I didn't realise you would have company.'

'Dick Foster,' Tessa said, equally cold. 'We were at university together, we were just renewing an old friendship.'

'Jolly for you,' he said.

'Yes, it was.' They stood in the little room glaring at each other like sworn enemies, and sparks seemed to sizzle in the air as grey eyes clashed with green.

Then Alaric said, 'I didn't come here to fight with you, Tessa,' and suddenly he looked infinitely weary, just as he had looked when he arrived last night.

'What did you come for then?' she asked with a level glance. Heaven forbid that she should give herself away again, as she had done on the heath. No more imagining she saw messages in his eyes that were merely the by-products of her own love and longing.

He drew in a long, harsh breath and burst out, 'I'm tired of all the pussyfooting, Tessa, of being scared of going too far, too soon.' His face was very pale, it had a drawn, haggard look that pulled at her heart. 'When you rejected me that night it hurt like hell, but I told myself it was my pride that was hurt and that I'd forget you pretty soon. It didn't work like that.' He made a small, helpless gesture.

'There hasn't been a moment when you haven't been in my mind,' he went on. 'And now I've got to tell you and risk it. I love you, Tessa, I want you so much it's sending me crazy, I'm no good without you. The new lab, the party tonight, everything will be——' he swallowed convulsively '—dust and ashes if I can't have you.'

He took a step towards her, held out his hands with an unsure, almost pleading gesture. 'Tessa?' he said.

She moved towards him like someone in a dream, and then their arms were round each other and he was holding her so tightly that it hurt, and the tears were rolling down her cheeks. She pressed her face against his thin shirt and the heat of his body sent shafts of quivering desire trembling through her.

Presently he released her and held her a little way away from him, and his voice was shaking as he said, very low, 'Tessa, this is more than I can handle. Will you—can we——'

She smiled up at him tremulously, green eyes glinting, all at once unafraid, her body responding with every nerve to the desperate need she saw in his face. 'My bed is very comfortable,' she said demurely, teasing as they had teased each other earlier in the day.

He gave a whoop of joy and triumph and turned the lock in the front door as she led the way upstairs. Her new dress was spread out on the bed and she hung it carefully over the back of a chair before she turned to see Alaric in the doorway, his smoky-grey eyes regarding her with such unashamed longing that she felt suddenly shy.

He had said, 'I love you,' and that was enough. She didn't know whether it was a pledge for the future, or just the heightened impulse of the moment, and she didn't care. She loved him with every fibre of her being and the future didn't exist. There were only the two of them together and the unbelievable thing that was happening.

Very slowly he came towards her. Very slowly he unbuttoned her blouse and pulled it off, leaving her breasts uncovered, the nipples hard and erect as he bent his head and his mouth caressed first one peak and then the other. Tessa's hand went to the fastening of her denim skirt and it slid to the floor so that she was only covered by a wisp of nylon and lace.

'You're so beautiful, my dearest, so incredibly beautiful,' Alaric groaned as he lifted her and laid her on the bed, her dark hair spread out against the whiteness of the pillow.

For a long moment he stood looking down at her and she met the stormy grey eyes as, with infinite care, he drew the final flimsy garment over her long, beautiful legs, and then such a wave of sheer erotic need took over that she arched herself towards him. 'Alaric—darling—please,' she pleaded and the next moment he had shed shirt and trousers and was on the bed beside her.

It was like nothing she had ever known or imagined. As his mouth and his hands explored every surface and every crevice of her, sensitively and expertly, the pleasure he gave her was close to pain, and the small moans she was hardly conscious of making increased the intensity of her pleasure. Her own fingers moved delicately over his strong, hard body, delighting in the contrast of smooth skin and rough hairiness, then digging convulsively into the hollows in his muscular shoulders as he moved above and against her, until she was almost at breaking point and cried out for fulfilment.

But still he delayed, savouring the taste of her skin, her mouth, and only when she was almost screaming with frustration did he thrust into her with a long groan of satisfaction. They clung together, skins damp as her legs wrapped round him, holding him close. 'I love you—love you——' he gasped out, his face buried in her neck as, almost immediately, the shattering climax took them both over the edge of the precipice at the same moment, and she cried the words back, all thought suspended as she reached the heights, and gradually floated down into a warm sea of pure happiness.

They stayed quiet then, their breathing gradually returning to normal. 'I knew it,' Alaric whispered exultantly. 'I knew it would be like this. You?'

'Wonderful,' murmured Tessa. 'The very best.'

He stroked her hair back from her face and looked down at her delicately flushed cheeks. 'Is that the truth?' he said quietly, and she nodded. 'The truth.'

He gazed at her for a moment longer then lowered his head and kissed her lingeringly. 'My lovely Tessa,' he said huskily, 'I've never heard more beautiful words. You're my woman now, aren't you? We can't let this go.'

'Oh, yes,' she whispered. 'I'm your woman.' She was his to do as he liked with, and she thrust away a tiny doubt that surfaced at the back of her mind, a doubt that said, 'For how long?'

Perhaps he sensed her momentary withdrawal from him, for he said quietly, 'Don't worry, love, it will be different this time, I'll make you forget that any other man existed,' and she knew what he was saying. He was perceptive, he must have guessed at some disappointment that would explain her earlier behaviour. Perhaps she should tell him about it, about Marc? But no, not now. It was so very complicated and it was all in the past. Let it stay there.

She snuggled up to him. 'I've forgotten already,' she said and heard his sigh of satisfaction as his arms closed round her again.

Much later Tessa went down and showered and made a fresh pot of tea and took it upstairs. She put the tray on the bedside table and slid back into bed, prodding Alaric's recumbent form. 'Have you forgotten that you're hosting a party in about half an hour?'

He rolled over, blinked and sat up. 'So I am,' he said. 'The host will have to be a trifle late, that's all.' He saw the tray. 'Tea—good. There's service for you. What a wife you're going to make, sweetheart.'

Tessa put down the teapot with a thud. 'Wife? You mean you want to marry me?'

Alaric grinned. 'I thought that was a condition of yours—like the old song, "Love and marriage go together like a horse and carriage." '

Tessa flushed. 'It wasn't a condition, it was a——'

'A defense?'

'Yes, I suppose so,' she mumbled. 'Anyway—I didn't—you can't accuse me of——'

'Holding out for marriage?' he chuckled. 'Perhaps not. But *I'm* doing just that. If you don't promise to marry me and put me out of my misery I'll—I'll chuck myself off the top of the cliff.' The smoke-grey eyes darkened, his voice changed as he took both her hands and looked deep into her eyes. 'I love you to distraction, there's nothing of value anywhere for me unless you're there to share it. You said you loved me—did you mean it?'

'Of course I meant it,' she told him. 'I've loved you ever since—oh, I can't remember, it seems so long ago. And of course I'll marry you. Tomorrow, if you like, only my nice mother would be disappointed. There's only one thing——' she added.

'What?' he rapped out anxiously.

'I'd been sort of looking forward to putting on a white coat again and working for Barney in the lab.'

He considered that. 'I might lend you to him for a week or two while I'm getting things organised at Head Office. That's something else I have to tell you, sweetheart, I'm doing my best to fix it up with my Mama to stay on here for another six months, to get the project really off the ground. That was what I phoned Cara about this morning, and she tells me that it's all arranged. How do you feel about that?'

'Marvellous!' Green eyes glinted up at him. 'I'll wear my white coat after all.'

'Temporarily only,' he warned. 'I shall need you to wear a white wedding dress very, very soon. You'll make a beautiful bride,' he went on dreamily. 'I can see you walking down the aisle to me on your father's arm. You must take me to see your parents very soon, love.' He took her face between his hands and kissed her slowly and would have gone on kissing her if she hadn't reminded him that he had to go back and change to receive his guests.

'Oh, God, yes,' he groaned. 'And my mama will be

arriving. Brace yourself, my love, you'll have to meet
her.' He chuckled. 'But her bark's worse than her
bite, as the saying goes, and she's going to be bowled
over when she sees you.'

He tossed off the last of his tea and pulled on shirt
and trousers. 'I'll come back for you, shall I?'

Tessa got behind him and pushed him gently down
the stairs and into the living-room. 'I've arranged to
come with the Clarks next door—*and* Dick Foster,'
she added mischievously, green eyes laughing into
his.

'Oh, have you indeed? Well, just so long as that
young oaf doesn't try to hold your hand in the back of
the car——' He drew her towards him. 'Do we really
have to go to this party?'

'Of course we do,' she said sternly. She reached up
and kissed him quickly and then ran back to the stairs.
Before he opened the front door he looked back.
'Tonight?' he added.

She nodded, half-way up the stairs. 'Tonight,' she
promised softly.

The big living-room in Alaric's apartment had been
transformed. There were roses everywhere—vases of
delicate pink buds on the white-clothed trestle tables
at the end of the room, pottery jugs full of blooms on
the desk and in the wide fireplace a great copper urn
was spilling out a blaze of scarlet, mixed with feathery
sprays of tamarisk, against the dark recess behind.

Tessa sought out Mrs Measures in the kitchen as
soon as she arrived. 'You've done wonders, Mrs M. It
all looks absolutely lovely.'

'It was me daughter picked the roses and did all the arranging, miss, she works in a flower shop in Bournemouth and knows about it. It does look nice though, doesn't it?' Mrs Measures, in a bright blue dress with a frilly pinafore tied round her ample waist, smiled happily through the doorway into the big room, which was quickly filling with guests. 'It's quite like the old days. I can just remember when there used to be parties in the house—when Mr Alaric's grandfather and grandmother were first married. I was only a wee girl then and my mother used to come to help the housekeeper, and she always came home with a great bunch of those red roses as Mr Alaric's grandmother had given her. A lovely lady she was. Of course, it's all different now, they used to have the parties in the big drawing-room downstairs—what they've turned into a laboratory.' She sighed, but then cheered up. 'But it's nice to think that the old house is still in the family like.'

Tessa looked down through the window at the rose-beds beyond the kitchen garden. In the spring she would come and do the pruning, she promised herself. Alaric would want to come here often, to keep an eye on his laboratory. Maybe they would even live here and he would commute to London. Her head filled with lovely plans.

Dick Foster spotted her as soon as she went out into the living-room. 'What are you having to drink, Tessa? There's lots of goodies over there—white wine, red wine, a sort of punch thing in a bowl with bits of orange floating on it; there's even a bottle or two of Scotch.' He leaned to her, whispering behind his hand, 'I expect that's for the bigwigs over there, not for us back-room boys. I'll go and get you a glass of wine.'

Barney stopped as he passed by. 'Hello, Tessa, you're looking great. See the mayor and mayoress over there——?' he leaned towards her confidentially '—and that's the registrar with them. We invited them so that they wouldn't be suspicious that we're going to blow the place up, or manufacture some awful poisons.' He grinned ruefully at her. 'I must go and reassure them.'

Tessa hadn't seen Alaric since she came in with the Clarks, but now she saw him across the room, his head way above those of the men in the group from the Town Hall. He saw her at the same moment, and their eyes met and her heart gave a great lurch. As Barney joined the group Alaric said a word of excuse and then he was moving across the room to where she stood by the wall.

She hadn't seen him in anything but casual clothes since that first interview but now he was wearing an immaculate grey suit and white shirt with a burgundy silk tie. He looked superb, she thought besottedly, her eyes drinking in every detail of him from his thick brown hair down to his well polished black shoes.

He paused in front of her. 'Hello,' he said softly, and his eyes looked into hers with wicked messages that sent thrills wriggling through her. 'You look gorgeous, I was right about the dress.'

She grinned up at him. 'You look very pretty yourself.'

'Don't I just?' He grinned back complacently,

fingering his shirt collar. 'But it's agony having to wear a tie on a warm night like this. Everything's going well, don't you think? We've got the town clerk here and the registrar and the mayor and mayoress, you must meet them all later on. My mama and Cara are staying at Blandford—they should be here at any moment. I'd better be at the front door to welcome Mama officially.'

He paused for a moment, frowning slightly, then said, 'We should be there together, Tessa, that's what I'd like. Only maybe it would be politic to announce our news to Mama in private, later in the evening.'

He leaned his head closer and his mouth touched her hair, but he wasn't caring who noticed and what conclusions they came to. 'This is a great occasion for me, my dearest,' he said, his voice low and husky, 'and having you makes it one I'll remember all my life. Wish me luck.'

She watched him walk away across the room and she thought that her heart would burst with love and pride. He was such a wonderful man, a big man, a man with ideas, a man who made things happen. And he loved her. *Tonight*, she whispered to herself, as Dick came back with her glass of wine. *Tonight*.

More guests arrived. Dick brought along the two young chemists who were to share the cottage with him to be introduced to Tessa. Husbands and wives of the new staff had been invited and soon the long room was full to overflowing. The windows were open but the June night was so warm that the air coming in did

little to cool the room. Talk and laughter and the clink
of glasses sent the decibels soaring up and down like
waves. Dick kept close to Tessa, and Tessa watched
the door where Alaric would appear with his
mother—and Cara Everett.

At last he came, holding his mother's arm, smiling.
Mrs Brent looked regal in a black couturier suit, an
enormous pearl brooch in the lapel, her grey hair
simply styled and immaculate. On Alaric's other side
Cara Everett was gaudy in comparison, in a pink silk
trouser-suit with applied glitter that caught the light,
dancing in hundreds of little stars. Tessa heard a low
wolf-whistle from some man behind her.

After that the proceedings were really under way.
Mrs Brent was introduced by Alaric and she made a
short, gracious speech of welcome. The mayor made a
longer speech, inserting the obligatory joke or two.
Then it was Barney's turn to announce that he would
later on be pleased to show guests round the
laboratory in small parties of five or six. Meanwhile,
he told them, it was very much cooler in the garden,
for anyone who cared to walk round and look at the
roses and the view of the sea. The crowd in the room
began to thin out as visitors made their way
downstairs.

Alaric was standing by the long white-clothed
trestle table with its decoration of pink roses, his
mother and Cara beside him. The new lab staff, who
had been politely holding back, were gathered near,
helping themselves to what remained of the savoury
bites on the table.

Tessa's heart began to thud as Alaric came over to her and took her arm, leading her back to the group beside the table.

'Mama, I want you to meet Tessa Durant.' There was a note in his voice that made Mrs Brent's keen, clever eyes rest on Tessa assessingly as she inclined her head with a murmured 'How d'you do.'

'And what is Tessa's role here, Alaric?' she enquired. Her expression, the amused quirk of one thin eyebrow, said everything that she hadn't said. *Your new girlfriend, I suppose?*

Cara Everett spoke then, for the first time. She looked round the group, which now included Barney and John and Sheila Clark. Then her cold blue gaze settled on Tessa with a look so venomous, so vindictive, that Tessa's stomach went hollow.

'Miss Durant is Alaric's new "find", isn't she, Alaric?' She smiled thinly. 'One of his special team here, engaged as research chemist, she tells me.' She turned to Alaric. 'What a pity you didn't go a little further into Miss Durant's past history, Alaric, you might not have taken her on so hastily if you'd troubled to find out why she left the last job she had in research with our subsidiary company, Ferris Knight.'

Suddenly the room was quiet. Nobody in the group around the table spoke. Cara Everett's gaze was fixed contemptuously, accusingly, on Tessa's ashen face. 'Why were you sacked, my dear? I was up at Ferris Knight's offices yesterday and the records I saw put it down as "Gross negligence and incompetence".' Her gaze swivelled round to Alaric, standing like a statue beside Tessa. 'Hardly a good recommendation for a top job in your new lab, Alaric dear.'

Through a grey haze that seemed to hover in front of her eyes Tessa heard Alaric's sharp intake of breath. She dared to glance up at his face and saw there the cold, merciless anger that she had seen there once before.

Sickly, she averted her eyes and saw Barney staring at her in disbelief. 'It's not true, Tessa? There's some mistake, surely?'

Dear Barney, Tessa thought, dear loyal Barney. Her mouth twisted into a travesty of a smile as she said in a clear, flat voice, 'I'm sorry, Barney, but it's true. It's quite true. Now, if you'll all excuse me, I think I'd like to leave.'

Blindly she pushed her way through the crowd to the door. Some of them would have witnessed that little drama, others not. She held her head high as she went; it didn't matter what any of them thought, she wouldn't be seeing them again.

It was Barney who came after her as she stumbled down the stairs. 'Tessa—wait. Don't just walk out like this.'

They were in the drive outside the front door now. 'Where are you going?' he urged worriedly. 'Let me take you back to the cottage.'

'Oh, thank you, Barney—if you would.' Tears were burning behind her eyes but she didn't let them escape. Tears would come later.

She had lost Alaric, he would never forgive her for

deceiving him, for subjecting him to this distasteful, embarrassing scene. But worst of all, she had spoilt the occasion that was to have been the crowning moment of his achievement.

For that she would never forgive herself.

CHAPTER NINE

BARNEY drove the Escort slowly along the lanes, as if Tessa were an invalid that he had to treat with care. Now and again he glanced sideways at her, frowning a little, and eventually he said tentatively, 'Tessa dear, I'm sure there's been some mistake. Won't you tell me about it?' but she shook her head dumbly and he sighed and drove on.

They were nearly back at the cottage when the sound of a car approaching from behind had Barney cursing and drawing in to the hedge. 'Bloody fool, going at that rate,' he growled and then, 'What the hell does he think he's doing?' as a large car overtook and pulled up abruptly in front of them, blocking the road.

Alaric jumped out and strode back to the Escort as Barney stamped on the brakes and swung open the driving-door, scowling. 'What's the big idea, Alaric? You nearly had me in the ditch.' He got out of the car and the two men confronted each other.

'Where do you think you're going?' Alaric ground out.

'Tessa wanted to go back to her cottage—I'm driving her there.'

'The hell you are,' said Alaric. 'Tessa's coming with me, we have things to talk about.'

The big man hesitated but Alaric had no time to spare for argument. He threw open the passenger door of the Escort and gripped Tessa's arm and she felt herself being pulled out of her seat, none too kindly, and bundled into the Jaguar, still panting gently in front.

'Sorry, Barney,' Alaric threw over his shoulder and the Jaguar moved off.

'Wh-what is this?' Tessa croaked. 'Where are you taking me?'

'Somewhere where we can be alone.'

She had heard that terrible flatness in his voice before and it hurt like a physical wound. She didn't speak again as Alaric drove, too fast, along the narrow roads. It was almost dark when the car turned in between high gates, passed one or two low wooden buildings and slid to a stop and she saw that they were in an enormous empty car park. In front of them there was nothing but gently rising sandhills sprouting with grasses and beyond that the vast mysterious expanse of the sea.

Alaric switched off the engine, and in the sudden silence Tessa began to tremble violently, but he made no move to comfort her.

She glanced up and saw the grimness in his face. 'I didn't think you'd want to see me again,' she faltered. 'I'm sorry about your party. I should have told you before.'

'Yes,' he said. 'You should. It was loathsome having to hear it like that, from that bitch of a woman.' The anger still lingered in his voice.

'But you came after me——' she ventured.

'I stopped long enough to set the record right for anyone who happened to be listening to that bit of melodrama, and to tell Cara Everett exactly what I thought of her,' he said. 'I doubt if she will be with our firm very much longer. I also put my mama's mind at rest concerning the girl I'm going to marry. I think you'll find her perfectly well disposed towards her prospective daughter-in-law when next you meet. She's wanted a grandson for some time.'

'I don't understand,' Tessa quavered. 'You don't have to marry me—you can't want a girl who's let you down—deceived you——' She was sobbing now. 'And you were so angry.'

'Not with you,' he said. 'I was livid with Cara for snooping up in Birmingham—which she admitted she did—and for choosing that moment and that despicable method of taking her revenge on me. What there was between us was over a long time ago and she knew that, but she wouldn't let go. I had it out with her this afternoon when she turned up at the lab again, and there were some unpleasant things said.'

His arm came out then and gathered her against him. 'Stop it, my love, stop it.' He bent and kissed her wet cheeks. 'I wasn't deceived. I knew the whole story. Cara wasn't telling me anything I didn't know already.'

'Then why——' Tessa began distractedly, but he put his fingers across her mouth. 'Shush, sweet, and let me explain.' He eased her more comfortably into the crook of his arm.

After a while he said, 'Remember that first time we met—at the interview? I couldn't get out of my mind the way you looked at me—as if you'd seen a ghost. The thing intrigued me. The old black magic really began to work then.'

Tessa stirred in his arms but said nothing.

'And when we were together I was falling more and more in love with you. Then you rejected me, that night before I went back to London, and I told myself I'd forget you, but of course I couldn't. You were there all the time, sending me crazy. I had to try to find out about you, there was such a lot that didn't seem to add up. I decided to do some detective work, so I went up to Birmingham, as you know. I found out that Tom Jarvis, who was head of your department when you worked there, had retired, and I sought him out and we had a long talk. He told me—everything I wanted to know.'

Tessa bit her lip hard. 'Oh, he shouldn't have done that. I asked him——'

'Jarvis is very fond of you, Tessa,' Alaric went on quietly. 'He knew that you and Marc Nichols were living together and that you lost your baby after the car accident that killed Marc. After Marc's death Jarvis discovered evidence that the mistake you were sacked for—and that cost the company more than a million pounds, by the way—wasn't yours at all but that you'd been covering up for Marc. Tom told me how he tried to persuade you to come clean about the whole thing and ask for your job back. But you refused. *Why*, Tessa? Was it because you still loved Marc Nichols, in spite of everything? In spite of the fact that he'd taken up with another girl, even when you were still living together? Oh, yes, Tom Jarvis told me that too. He thinks a lot of you, you know, he was very angry on your behalf but he felt he couldn't interfere, when you pleaded with him not to.'

Tessa shook her head in utter weariness. 'Do we have to go through all this again?'

Her fingers were lacing themselves together on her lap and Alaric gripped them hard and said, 'I think we do, my darling. I'm sorry, but I have to know.'

When she was silent he urged again, *Do* you still love him, Tessa? Was that why you still needed to protect him, even after his death?'

She closed her eyes and said slowly. 'No, it wasn't because I still loved Marc. He killed that love when he wanted me to kill our baby. But I felt that what had happened was my own fault—I knew what I was doing when I agreed to take the blame. Oh, it was all such a mess.' Her voice trembled and broke. 'I knew I should have told you, I felt guilty about accepting the job you offered. I tried to tell you once or twice but I was afraid——' She shuddered violently.

'Afraid of losing the job?'

'At first,' she said, very low. 'And afterwards—I was afraid you'd—you'd think badly of me.'

His laugh was a broken sound. He drew her closer against him and stroked her hair as her head lay against his shoulder. 'I'm sorry, my darling girl, to have to rake all this up, but I had to know. In a twisted sort of way I was jealous.'

She looked up at his face, shadowy in the dimness of the car. 'Jealous? Of a man who's dead? Of a man you never knew?'

He said grimly, 'I saw Marc Nichols' record. There was a photograph of him attached to it. It might almost have been a photograph of me. It shook me rigid, and it explained quite a lot.'

He reached over and opened the car door. 'I think we both need some air,' he said.

They walked over the deserted sandhills towards the sea. Tessa's knees felt weak and shaky but Alaric's arm was round her, guiding her surely over the bumps and hollows of soft grassy sand. When they reached the margin of the tide she paused, looking down at the dark water edged with creamy white where the waves turned gently over, taking deep breaths to relax her tense muscles. They stopped together, arms round each other, looking out to sea. Above, the sky was dark now and the stars pinpoints of light. Then, with dramatic suddenness, the crescent of a new moon pierced the horizon, rose higher and higher as they watched, until it sailed clear, brilliant and serene in a black velvet sky.

Tessa drew in her breath. 'Incredible,' she murmured.

Alaric bent his head and his mouth found hers. 'Our very own moon,' he whispered against her lips. 'Remember the last one?'

'When we were grovelling in the mud beside the barn?' They both laughed and the old unhappiness seemed to lift a little.

She turned her head to look at Alaric. The moonlight threw shades on to the hollows in his lean cheeks and his hair was ruffled in the warm breeze, and he seemed to her the most wonderful man in all the world. Many women must have loved him, but she was the one he wanted to marry.

She said, 'Cara Everett told me you and she were lovers—had been for a long time. She was warning me off.'

Alaric muttered something highly uncomplimentary. 'That woman—she never gives up. 'Were you jealous?' he added hopefully.

'Disgustingly,' Tessa told him.

Alaric laughed softly. 'Good! That evens things up a bit.'

She looked down at the waves that broke lazily at their feet.

'Why didn't you tell me when you came back that you knew—about Marc?' she asked.

'Because I was scared stiff,' Alaric said ruefully.

'You—scared? Don't give me that.'

'I was, you know. I was deeply in love with you and I had to be sure you loved me—not a ghost. I thought—if you let me love you I'd know.'

She nodded thoughtfully. That explained so much. Answered so many questions. She said, 'But what we have is so very different—things I never had with Marc. Friendship. Trust. Oh—so much more. It's you I love, Alaric. Darling, darling Alaric. I think I've been searching all my life for you.' She pressed the softness of her body close to him, burying her head against his chest. 'Are you convinced?'

He lifted her chin and kissed her mouth and the salty taste of the sea was on his lips. 'Almost,' he said and she felt him tremble against her. 'Let's go back to the cottage now, and you can finish the job.'

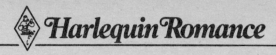
Harlequin Romance

Coming Next Month

#2965   NO GREATER JOY   Rosemary Carter
Alison fights hard against her attraction to Clint, driven by
bitter memories of a past betrayal. However, handsome,
confident, wealthy Clint Demaine isn't a man to take no for
an answer.

#2966   A BUSINESS ARRANGEMENT   Kate Denton
When Lauren advertises for a husband interested in a businesslike approach to marriage, she doesn't expect a proposal from a
handsome Dallas attorney. If only love were part of the
bargain....

#2967   THE LATIMORE BRIDE   Emma Goldrick
Mattie Latimore expects problems—supervising a lengthy
engineering project in the Sudan is going to be a daunting
experience. Yet heat, desert and hostile African tribes are
nothing compared to the challenge of Ryan Quinn. (More about
the Latimore family introduced in THE ROAD and TEMPERED
BY FIRE.)

#2968   MODEL FOR LOVE   Rosemary Hammond
Felicia doesn't want to get involved with handsome financial
wizard Adam St. John—he reminds her of the man who once
broke her heart. So she's leery of asking him to let her sculpt
him—it might just be playing with fire!

#2969   CENTREFOLD   Valerie Parv
Helping her twin sister out of a tight spot seems no big deal to
Danni—until she learns she's supposed to deceive
Rowan Traynor, her sister's boyfriend. When he discovers the
switch his reaction is a complete surprise to Danni....

#2970   THAT DEAR PERFECTION   Alison York
A half share in a Welsh perfume factory is a far cry from Sophie's
usual job as a model, but she looks on it as an exciting
challenge. It is unfortunate that Ben Ross, her new partner,
looks on Sophie as a gold digger.

Available in March wherever paperback books are sold, or
through Harlequin Reader Service:

In the U.S.
901 Fuhrmann Blvd.
P.O. Box 1397
Buffalo, N.Y. 14240-1397

In Canada
P.O. Box 603
Fort Erie, Ontario
L2A 5X3

Harlequin Superromance

**Here are the longer, more involving stories you
have been waiting for...Superromance.**

Modern, believable novels of love, full of the complex
joys and heartaches of real people.

Intriguing conflicts based on today's constantly
changing life-styles.

Four new titles every month.
Available wherever paperbacks are sold.

SUPER-1

Keepsake

 Harlequin Books

You're never too young to enjoy romance. Harlequin for you . . . and Keepsake, young-adult romances destined to win hearts, for your daughter.

Pick one up today and start your daughter on her journey into the wonderful world of romance.

Two new titles to choose from each month.

ADULTB-1

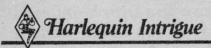
Harlequin Intrigue

Two exciting new stories each month.

Each title mixes a contemporary, sophisticated romance with the surprising twists and turns of a puzzler...romance with "something more."

Because romance can be quite an adventure.

Intrg-1

Romance, Suspense and Adventure

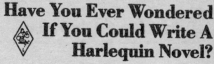

Have You Ever Wondered If You Could Write A Harlequin Novel?

Here's great news—Harlequin is offering a series of cassette tapes to help you do just that. Written by Harlequin editors, these tapes give practical advice on how to make your characters—and your story—come alive. There's a tape for each contemporary romance series Harlequin publishes.

Mail order only

All sales final

TO: *Harlequin Reader Service*
Audiocassette Tape Offer
P.O. Box 1396
Buffalo, NY 14269-1396

I enclose a check/money order payable to HARLEQUIN READER SERVICE® for $9.70 ($8.95 plus 75¢ postage and handling) for EACH tape ordered for the total sum of $_____*
Please send:

☐ Romance and Presents   ☐ Intrigue
☐ American Romance   ☐ Temptation
☐ Superromance   ☐ All five tapes ($38.80 total)

Signature_____

Name:_____
                                                             (please print clearly)

Address:_____

State:_____ Zip:_____

*Iowa and New York residents add appropriate sales tax.

                                                                           AUDIO-H